Fiona and the Sailor

by

Jeanette Collins

Fiona and the Sailor

Cover Art by *The Wild Rose Press, Inc.*

The Wild Rose Press, Inc.
PO Box 708
Adams Basin, NY 14410-0708
Visit us at www.thewildrosepress.com

Publishing History
First Edition, 2023
Trade Paperback ISBN 978-1-5092-5211-4
Digital ISBN 978-1-5092-5212-1

Published in the United States of America

The banker took a folder and withdrew a paper.

"I imagine my account is now worth quite a bit, after ten years," she said hopefully.

He glanced up with a pained expression. "Miss Seymour, I cannot give you your funds."

Fiona's blood chilled. "Why ever not?"

"The monies were withdrawn, ma'am, one month ago. By a Viscount Greathouse."

Everything went numb, her feet, her hands, her brain.

"This gentleman is known to you?" he asked in a courteous voice.

She caught a breath. "My f-father. He took it. He knew I would come, and he took it." She had to get away, run, get out of this building, and stood. "The book, please."

He handed it back. Fiona rushed from the office and across the marble lobby, her steps echoing. Pushing past others, she stumbled toward the great doors. Gone. He stole it! Stole it! Tears choked her throat as Fiona despaired. What could she do with no money? Where could she go? Home? Back home?

People moved aside, and she hurried headlong through the great doors, the valise dragging her down. The toe of her half boot caught; she tripped, fell forward, and hit her head on the sidewalk.

Previous Releases from Jeanette Collins

The Gamble
Found Christmas

Chapter One

London, Sunday, May 7, 1815

Fiona hesitated outside the library door. The unexpected summons boded ill. Which of her errors had been discovered? She smoothed her pink-striped muslin morning gown and tapped.

His voice resounded. "Come."

She turned the knob and stepped in, the room airless and dim, the curtains drawn closed. A single lamp spilled a puddle of light, making dark voids and ominous channels in his face.

"Shut the door," her father commanded. "Sit down."

Fiona sat in the enormous chair before his massive walnut desk. Her feet dangled. Her heart thumped.

He replaced the pen in its ebony stand and folded his hands, the gold rings on his fingers gleaming dully. "Word has reached me, obstinate girl," he scolded, "that last evening you declined to dance with Lord Cameron."

She felt some relief. "Not exactly, Father. The truth is—my slipper—"

He shook his shaggy ginger head, his mouth a tight line. "There is no excuse for such incivility." He leaned forward, elbows on the desk, his chin doubling. "I have just now spoken with his representative. The earl has been gracious enough to overlook your lack of courtesy, and you may be thankful for that." He steepled his blunt fingers and grinned smugly. "You may care to learn the gentleman has offered for you, and I have agreed to his suit."

Fiona gasped in shock.

"It is an honor most extreme," he gloated. "It will open doors, both financial and social. As a broker, Cameron is vastly rich and well-placed at only five-and-thirty. You will enjoy high status, as will I." He assumed a faraway meditation, and his small eyes glittered. "Accepted in every house of standing and at court, I shall amass greater powers."

Fiona nervously clasped her hands. "But, truly, this cannot be. He does not know me! I do not know him."

"That is of no consequence. It will come. You have breeding, your late grandmother a cousin of the king. An association will do credit to everyone. As Lord Greathouse, I have distinguished myself," he continued, fingering his showy diamond cravat pin, "as few have done before me." He waved his hand carelessly. "Go on your way now. I am occupied."

She *must* take a stand. "Father, if I may say, I have no wish to marry, and certainly not to Lord Cameron."

Her father bent to his papers. "Send in Quiggs as you go."

"Perhaps he is mistaken," Fiona pleaded, "and will change his mind. If we meet."

His expression became feral. He showed his teeth, his black eyes blazed. She trembled.

"Do you imagine," he thundered, "that I will deign to keep you in the goddamned luxury of my house and my name? Pampered and cosseted, while you do nothing to afford me gain? Pay for another season and garb you in a ransom to draw attention?" he shouted. "Am I to sink into poverty with you on my neck, an unwanted spinster? No! You shall marry Cameron promptly and had best make him appreciate the bargain, because you will not return here! Now, get out."

Fiona stood, her legs shaking, and shuffled to the door.

"And send in Quiggs!" he bellowed.

Quiggs, his sallow face empty of emotion, watched as she passed him in the hall, his arm full of folders and documents. Fiona dashed away to the stairs, up to her room, locked the door, and sat down by the window. Her mind jostled with fear, sorrow, and desperation.

Only nineteen, Fiona had hoped she had more time. At least this one last season, before being sold off for whatever her father perceived as useful. Namely money and social advantage. The highest bidder was Cameron, it seemed. Fiona had evaded the rest of them, danced away, rudely avoided, was inane, stupidly chattered, fell icily silent, anything to discourage unwanted suitors. She had even lied outrageously to rid herself of the dogged Lord Wilton, who owned a racing stable and was offensive in manner and dress.

Then Cameron had come along, a man sixteen years her elder. Fiona had not disliked him quite so much as his predecessors, because in his company she had felt absolutely nothing. Not tolerance, dislike, or friendship, just—nothing. He hung about, his voracious gaze on her, and she had begun to endure a creeping despair. Last evening at the Stanfords' ball, he had put an unwelcome hand on her arm and requested the next waltz. Fiona had immediately feigned discomfort and limped to the retiring room. She lingered there until she could escape to her carriage.

Of course, he knew she had snubbed him. His revenge? Marry her and drag her off to his cave, like a caught rabbit. Too negligent and heartless to come in person, he sent his *representative*! Some fellow like Quiggs.

Fiona sat quietly as the sunlight shifted in the poplar trees, illuminating green and gold new leaves. Soon the budding roses would burst into fragrant bloom. Day lilies and blue iris were pushing through the warm soil. The new tulip bulbs she had planted last year would spring up to fill in gaps in the flower garden that she loved. She would not be here to see it. She intended to run away.

Energized, she hopped up. In her dressing room, she unlocked a small compartment below a shelf. This held an old tin soapbox ornamented with embossed flowers, and she opened the dented lid. It contained her life savings and, best of all, the passbook to an account at the Bank of England willed to her by her mother.

Fiona treasured the small booklet and imagined the amount had grown over the last ten years. It was a legacy of her mama's love, and with it, Fiona could support a flight for freedom. As much as she could buy with the balance, plus seventeen shillings, eight pence in cash.

She locked the box away and replaced the key in her stocking drawer. Now she must formulate a plan.

****

Fiona went down for lunch wearing a placid face. Her father glared at her over his meal. She labored to appear mindless, which he assumed she was anyway.

Presently, he amused himself with tales of his glory.

"You will be glad to hear, Fiona, that I received praise for my suggestion of new rules for White's. We simply must crack down on the lowering of the bar for membership. The war has allowed the proper rules adhered to by gentlemen to grow slack. I intend to put a stop to that."

He gulped his wine and waited for admiration.

Fiona replied, "Ah?"

Her father groomed his self-love like a cat. "Without conscientious members such as myself to man the ramparts, we would be invaded by the lower classes. Cousins, friends of friends, and the like. Complete loss of distinction there. I will not endure it and said so. Gregg, more wine. Look sharp, man! My glass is dry."

The footman rushed to obey. Fiona ate asparagus and cold beef and thought of Scotland, a wild country full of robust savages. Perhaps she need not go that far. Distance posed a problem, since Father would send bloodhounds after her, his prime investment. She represented all those lavish gowns and slippers, emblems of his sacrifice. Therefore, she must pay it all back for a lifetime.

Her resentment multiplied. Curses if she would. She would eat it all up like this beef and disappear, to be swallowed by the world. The romance of it, the rebellion, filled her heart with strength.

She enjoyed a dish of flan and plotted her escape. Sunday afternoons, her father went to White's for cards and to harass other members to adopt his views. Fiona would go back to the musty library and study English maps. She needed a destination. Somewhere agreeable, not too distant to reach, far enough not to be found. A place she had no connection to. The idea grew. Not Brighton or Bristol, she hummed to herself.

True to his schedule, Father left the house at one of the clock, and Fiona hastened to the library. She took down a volume of maps and boldly sat at her father's desk to study them. The shadowy images lacked sufficient detail, but she could discern that Surrey might do. The distance from London did not look too great, and she knew not a soul there.

She envisioned a tiny cottage in a village where she would be accepted as just another person. Then Fate would be her guide. She spent a pleasant hour in these dreams, then Sumpter peered in the open door.

"Your pardon, Miss Fiona, but you have a caller. Lord Cameron."

Her heart sank to the worn carpet. The butler exhibited a corner of sympathy. Of course, he knew, all the servants knew she had been sold.

"Thank you, Sumpter. I will be right along." She replaced the book of maps, amassed courage, and marched to the drawing room.

There Cameron stood. They were of similar height, but he was chubby. His cheeks were ruddy, his hair mouse brown. She judged he would soon grow fatter. In his starched cravat and lace-trimmed lawn shirt, he seemed girlish. The lie was put to this when he boomed in a baritone, "My dear Miss Seymour, how fine you appear today."

"Will you not sit down, your lordship?"

"Thank you." He plopped into a Louis chair.

"Tea? A brandy?"

"No, we have matters to discuss." He took papers

from his coat and unfolded them. "I received with gratitude your father's gracious permission to begin a courtship and wished to apprise you of my demands."

She took a seat. "Sir?"

"What I require of a wife."

Fiona strove to remain civil. "Allow me to say—"

He raised a staying hand. "I have no doubt you will be submissive to all my wants. That is a given. Nonetheless, I wish to be clear in all matters that evolve between us. Number one. You will—"

Fiona's cheeks burned in resentment. "No, my lord, I will not. Not any of it. My father may have informed you he would accept your attentions, but I was not consulted. I contend the arrangement has nothing to do with me."

His manner did not alter. The oaf thought himself a catch and that she was being foolishly stubborn. "Now, now," he cooed. "I am aware you have a streak of willfulness, shall we say, and I applaud that in an unmarried lady of rank. However, as my wife, all that must, of course, cease."

Fiona measured her words. "Your lordship, this is all wrong. You do not love me. I do not, and never shall, love you."

He became cautious, narrowing his gaze. "There is another man?"

"Yes!" she exclaimed, glad for an out, and placed a hand on her bosom. "My heart is given away, sir. I am so sorry."

Cameron smirked. "You will forget him."

"Not likely." Fiona had enough of this. "Listen with care. My father has no interest in me or my life. None. I am a pawn, as you will also be if you pursue this ill-advised notion. He desires to profit from your title, your money, and your influence, and to be rid of me. Begone, sir. Find someone to truly care for, who will care for you."

His pale brown eyes turned flinty. "What about what *I* want? I want your youth and beauty for my own."

"Everyone sensible is aware those qualities will not last."

"I will take them while they do."

Fiona stood. "I cannot agree, now or ever. Our conversation is over. I would ask you to leave, Lord Cameron."

Standing to face her, he became more mean than pudgy. "This is not done! I have your father's signature. You are legally obligated and *will* be mine."

Fiona smiled. "Not if I kill myself first." With that, she left him standing there. In the foyer, Sumpter quickly stood away from the doors, all innocence.

"Please show his lordship out, Sumpter, if you will."

"This way, Lord Cameron," the butler urged, as the nuisance waddled toward her.

"I will return tomorrow to speak further with your father, Miss Seymour," he squealed. "Then we shall see where we stand. Know that I always get what I want. Always."

Fiona did not speak. He reached for her hand, and she backed away. Sumpter shoved his hat and stick at Cameron and opened the front door. The idiot snuffled and walked out. The door closed, and she leaned on the wall.

"Thank you, Sumpter."

The lean, narrow-faced butler bowed. "Yes, miss. Any time, any occasion, I will strive to be of assistance."

"I will need it. Soon, I believe," Fiona added, trudged to the stairs and up to her room. He would come back tomorrow. Time had grown short. Must think, must plan, but she already felt terribly burdened.

Fiona surveyed the room where she had grown up. Her father's idea of luxury consisted of old pieces of furniture gleaned from refurbished public rooms. Nothing matched. Under her bed, the Turkey rug had a burn hole in it the size of a meat platter. The glass above her makeshift dressing table, formerly a hall writing desk, bore a foggy haze. Marry or be cast out of this palace? She could not wait to leave, just not with Cameron.

In her spacious dressing room hung clothing galore, suitable for all occasions. She must be seen, like prize poultry, so fancy feathers were required. Fiona assembled suitable sturdy gowns and accessories, making a pile on the bed. This built up and shrank again, since she would have to carry it all herself.

Betimes, she considered her destination. London and its environs were all she knew. A move across the Thames and into Surrey seemed feasible on the map. One of the villages along the water would be highly pleasant. Expenses would be low, unlike in larger towns. No one would dream of looking for her there.

A friend once mentioned her brother had gone to one of the larger inns to catch the mail coach to Winchester. A ticket could be purchased at such a place. The more Fiona thought of it, the more plausible it seemed. She would make her money last and create a life for herself.

Father did not come home for dinner, which suited everyone. The buxom older maid, Daisy, dashed about, and Gregg, the footman, served her meal, both the picture of cheer. The food was good, and Fiona had two glasses of Burgundy, which lifted her spirits greatly. Dessert was a slice of butter cake, and she enjoyed coffee.

When her mother lived, Fiona had thought the table happy, but perhaps the happiness had been hers alone. Mama was pensive. Father was talkative but said nothing anyone wanted to hear. Then one April day, Mama had fallen in the back yard and died. Dr. Calvert said her heart had stopped, and Fiona had puzzled as to what that meant. Had Mama been sad? Did that make hearts stop? She had not found an answer.

Fiona went up the back stairs, along the upper hall to the box room, and extracted a brown leather valise. It was part canvas and not too heavy. She tucked it away in her room as Daisy appeared at the door, her friendly face jovial, her graying hair a mass of ringlets.

"Here I am, miss, to help."

"Thank you, Daisy. I would like a bath."

"I will see to it. Such a nice gown this," she remarked as she unhooked Fiona's stays.

"It is. I can do the rest, if you will see to the bath water."

The maid left to do her double duties, Father unwilling to hire a lady's maid. More of her missing luxuries. Daisy worked night and day, bless her. Fiona took off her clothes and laid them aside. In her robe, she gazed out at the darkened sky and a few small stars, then was seized by a flock of uncertainties. If she did not take *everything*, all her clothes and slippers, this warm robe, her favorite things, where could she find comfort? That would be the task, to make new comforts for herself.

The water arrived with Daisy and Gregg, and her bath was prepared.

Alone, Fiona sank into the water. It would not be easy, this anticipated venture, but if she stayed, it would be a whole lot worse.

Fiona finished at last and donned a fresh nightie. The bath was removed, and she climbed into her bed. Goodnights said, Daisy extinguished the lamps and departed.

Fiona liked the dark and the quiet, went over her imprecise plans, and satisfied, relaxed into the warmth of her covers. She conjured a dream of a new life, true friends, and a place to be at home. Tears filled her eyes. A real home, with people who loved her. Where she mattered and had something to do to make them happy. She whispered, "Mama," closed her eyes, and waited for sleep. After a time, it came.

****

Monday

Fiona woke before the first light, quickly dressed, and closed the valise. She took her money and account book from the tin box and replaced the box in the compartment below the shelf, leaving the key inside. The valuables went into her reticule along with her pearwood comb, a dozen hairpins, and two hankies.

She stood by her door, listening, the valise in hand. It was not too heavy; she could manage it and crept down the hall to the stairs, the house nearly silent. Faint noises came from the kitchens, along with the smell of coffee brewing. Fiona slid back the iron bolt on the door, opened it, and slipped through. Silently closed it again and dashed away, the valise bumping her leg. She made it the block along Green Street to Park Lane and paused there to catch her breath.

The early morning was already busy with traffic; carriages and carts swept along noisily. Fiona, an old hand at this, raised her arm. A hackney rattled up and stopped for her. She heaved in the valise and instructed the scruffy driver, who squinted curiously at her.

"Threadneedle Street, and the Bank of England, please."

"Get yerself in," he called, "afore we be run down."

She climbed up, the vehicle smelling of wet wool. They rolled along over the cobbles, Fiona conscious of her freedom. All was going well. Father would soon realize she had gone and gnash his teeth in rage. There could be no doubt why she had left.

They reached the stately bank, and Fiona stepped down. On tiptoes, she handed the jarvey a coin. "Perhaps you would wait?" she asked.

He adjusted his tall hat. "Missy, it be a busy time. Take yer lot, and I can wait, unless someuns comes along needs a ride."

Fiona hauled out the valise, gathered her resolve, and entered the imposing establishment.

A man in a fine suit of clothes rose from his desk to welcome her. "Good day, miss. How may we serve you?"

"I wish to see about my account."

"Certainly. Come this way. You may leave your case here, if you like. It will be safe."

"Thank you."

She followed him to an inner office and another fellow. "This is Mr. Chartwell," he said as the tallish, very thin man stood. "He handles our private accounts."

"Good morning, miss?"

"Fiona Seymour."

"Please have a seat."

She presented her account book. "I wish to withdraw these funds."

He took the book and perused it. "One of our older accounts."

"Yes. Left me by my late mother."

"Stiles," he called. "Bring me the Seymour accounts."

In came a man with folders. Mr. Chartwell took one and withdrew a paper.

"I imagine it is now worth quite a bit, after ten years," Fiona said hopefully, as seconds passed.

Chartwell glanced up with a pained expression. "Miss Seymour, I cannot give you your funds."

Her blood chilled. "Why ever not?"

"The monies were withdrawn, ma'am, one month ago. By a Lord Greathouse."

Everything went numb, her feet, her hands, her brain.

"This gentleman is known to you?" he asked in a courteous voice.

She caught a breath. "My f-father. He took it. He knew I would come, and he took it." She had to get away, run, get out of this building, and stood. "The book, please."

He handed it back.

Fiona rushed from the office and across the marble

lobby, her steps echoing. She grabbed the valise and pushing past others, stumbled toward the door, the case hurting her leg. Gone. He stole it! *Stole* it! Tears choked her throat as Fiona despaired. What could she do with no money? Where could she go? Home? Back home?

People moved aside, and she hurried headlong through the great doors, the valise dragging her down. The toe of her half boot caught; she tripped, fell forward, and hit her head on the sidewalk.

****

Philip Laughton spent a tiresome hour at the bank, reviewing documents and signing papers. So, it was all his. Unexpected. Unwanted. He hastened through the lobby, rudely jostled by a woman carrying a clumsy valise. He reached the doors just as the creature sprawled headlong, face down on the sidewalk. Off went her little twist of a hat, exposing a tumble of reddish hair. He stepped closer to help. Damn, she had hit her head.

A knot of people gathered. The fellow from the bank stepped out, several ladies chittered. Concerned, Philip bent down. "Miss?"

The female sprang to life, rolled over nimbly, and stood up. Staggered, brushed off her clothing, and swayed.

He reached out, taking her arm. "Are you well? I believe you hit your—"

She pulled away. "Fine, I am fine. So sorry. So very sorry." She reached for her case and nearly toppled over sideways.

He steadied her, raised an arm, dizzy himself, and a hackney stopped at the curb.

"Yes," she whispered, "my hackney." Her eyes, a

mix of greens, rolled around drunkenly.

Philip picked up the valise, threw it in with her hat, and assisted her inside. He climbed in, winded, and took deep breaths.

She pokered up. "This is my hackney, sir. Please get out."

"Actually, ma'am, it is *my* hackney. I could not leave you on the sidewalk, and I badly needed to sit down."

Bloody hell, she tried to jump out again and cracked his knee with the damned valise. He winced in pain and pushed her away.

"You were sent by my father!" she accused, those eyes full of fire. Her straight brows dipped into a frown. Her nose wrinkled, rearranging a scattering of freckles. Her face heart-shaped, her full lips were a rosy pink.

"I will not go back!" she hotly insisted. "He has taken my money, the thief, but I will find a way." She glared at him with distaste. "You pitiful scoundrel, to do such low work. You pushed me, or I would not have fallen." She waved her arm. "Now you have lured me into this vehicle!"

He sat back. "Hush. I have not the strength to lure a stray puppy. I did *not* push you. You stumbled and went down like a dead tree, all on your own." He glanced over her. What a pretty dolly. "So, minx, you are on the run, eh? A lover is after you?"

"Certainly not! I am an independent person." She regarded him like he smelled bad. "What did he tell you? What horrid lies?"

Philip knocked on the roof. The hatch swung open. "Aye?"

"Take me—" He glanced at her. "—*us*, to a good

15

place for a breakfast."

"Aye, sir." The hatch flew shut.

"I am starved," he told her. "Likely you have not eaten. I wager little girls who run off seldom stop for a meal."

She fell silent as the vehicle moved along the street, her manner hopeless.

"We can have some food," he remarked, "then you can be on your way. Where are you off to?"

"I will not say," she huffed, "since you will tell *him*."

He had no patience left for this. "Listen well, my friend. I am in no one's employ. I finished my business, and now must eat. If you are hungry, I will feed you, inasmuch as you said your money was gone. Otherwise, you may depart when you will, valise, hat, and all."

The woman snatched up her hat, crushed it on her tresses, and studied him. "Is this true?" she murmured. "Or are you a kidnapper? You shall not frighten me. My father will pay to have me back. He has to, since I am bargained away," she exclaimed, raising her chin. "You look like a poor man. I will give you, um, five shillings to let me go."

Jesus, Philip thought, the imp was daffy. "Tempting," he replied, "but as I said, get out when you will. It is nothing to me. At the moment, my mind is on my belly, if I may be so indelicate."

She raised slender fingers to her forehead. "Is it bleeding?" she quietly asked, her green eyes wide.

"No, but it is dirty." He took out his pocket flask, dampened his handkerchief, and wiped off her forehead as she gaped. He showed her the soiled cloth. "See?"

"Oh. Thank you."

He took a swig. "Waste of good brandy."

She stared.

Fiona could scarcely believe what was happening, riding alone in a vehicle with the strangest man she had ever met. Very big, long legs, wide shoulders in a dark blue coat like sailors wear. Black leather trousers, big boots, large hands. A blue knitted hat over his hair and mocking eyes. Let him laugh at her predicament, she fumed, which he may indeed know nothing of. Thank God for that.

The hackney halted outside a coaching inn, the Weeping Damsel. How fitting. Her stomach growled. He smiled.

"Yes," she admitted, "I have not eaten today."

"So I hear."

Fiona gave way. "If you would buy me a cup of tea and perhaps a toast, I would be very grateful."

"Glad to do so."

He opened the door and stepped down, his expression strained. Was he hurt? In pain? He seemed tired out. Fiona felt a twinge of sympathy. He had been kind to her. He reached up to help her down and their gaze met. His observation was so direct, she felt a tremor and, shaken, glanced away. The result of this was she missed the step and fell out.

"Zounds," he yelled, catching her. "You will be the death of me."

She found her feet. He took the valise, paid the driver, clutched her arm, hustled her to the door and inside.

"Table," he barked to a waiter, who leapt to show them one. Fiona trailed along and, at his bidding, sat down. He sank heavily into a chair and took off his cap.

17

"Menu."

The waiter scurried to provide cards. Fiona took one, suddenly ravenous.

"Three whipped eggs," he chanted, "these potatoes, bacon rashers, and a slice of this ham. Whatever fruit is available. Lots of coffee." He looked to her.

"Um. One boiled egg and toast, please. Coffee would be lovely."

"Give her some bacon, and the potatoes," he added. "She could use a little meat on her."

The waiter scribbled. "Yes, sir."

Fiona glared. How dare he? She squeezed her hands together in her lap. Must be calm. He was paying, and she must save her coins. She took the moment to really look at him. The man was huge, had a black stubbly beard growth and longish black hair. Tanned skin. Skeptical dark eyes and a soft, wide mouth. Below his eyes were circles of weariness.

Fiona made conversation. "It was very good of you to help me."

"Hmmm."

"I think you have been ill?" she ventured.

"Was that a question?"

"Yes. You seem rather fatigued."

"I am."

He had not taken off his blue coat. Below it was a coarse linen shirt, buttoned to the throat. His hands were tanned, too, and looked strong. The coffee came. Fiona added a lump of sugar, and a dash of cream. He took his black.

"May I ask your name?"

"Philip."

She stirred her cup. "I am Fiona."

"Ho, Fiona, princess of the sidewalk."

"Ho, Philip, of the sly wit."

He laughed, a rumble in his chest.

It made her cross. "I know you think I am stupid, but I had a plan. It is just…my rightful inheritance has been stolen from me."

He raised a dark brow. "From the, my God, Bank of England?"

"Boldly stolen, sir, by my greedy, unprincipled father."

"Indeed?" he asked, sipping his coffee. "How much was involved?"

"Five hundred pounds," she declared, "plus ten years interest."

He glanced at his silverware. "Oh, well."

Fiona was freshly annoyed. "It is a fortune to me, sir, I will have you know. My entire future!"

"If the future consists of a sennight," he remarked.

The nerve of the man! The food arrived on steaming plates. He rapidly dug in, eating voraciously. She cracked the egg and took a bite. Nothing had been wrong with his stomach, whatever he had been ill with. Without the cap, his black hair was thick. He was rather handsome. Rugged. Muscular. If one liked that sort of thing.

"Were you in the war?" she inquired, buttering her toast.

"The whole world is in the war," he answered, chewing. He washed that down with his coffee and signaled imperiously for more. The waiter scampered to serve him.

"I presume you were on the side of England?" she irritably persisted.

"Correct."

Fiona ate her food, forgot about him, and brooded over what she should do. Walk back in the house as if nothing had happened? By now, Daisy had missed her when she had no breakfast and would come looking to find her. Father would descend from his lair and explode in fury. Mercy. They would all imagine she had been away for the entire night. Was she ruined?

She had never—well, seldom—disobeyed. This time would seal her doom. Even Cameron would not want her now. Fiona was cheered by this thought, but Father would find another fool with money and influence. They were all over the place.

It was a terrible predicament. Her forehead hurt. She could hide the valise, say she had gone out for an early walk and fallen down. Then had been rescued by—Fiona glanced up. Him? This Philip? Father would likely refuse him entrance, in his blue coat and heavy boots. And Cameron would be waiting.

The idea struck her. He could pose as her mystery lover! Cameron would foam over at the sight this large, arrogant man. She smiled.

"If you have overspent on this meal, I could give you what money I possess. I realize you are possibly um, in some need, or so it seems. If you would do something for me, only a small thing, I would give you all I have."

He drank his coffee, his fathomless eyes on her. "All you have, eh?"

"Oh, yes. Absolutely. Everything."

He grinned, the devil. "I will take it. Finish your food."

Would he do it? Time was passing. "Well, I rather

thought—"

He leaned toward her. "We have a bargain, do we not? Or are you reneging? Fie. Women cannot hold to a deal."

"Of course we can. I mean what I say, or I would not say it."

He summoned the waiter, searched his pockets, and came up with a sixpence. He casually flipped it to the surprised fellow, and pulled on the knitted cap. "Shall we go?"

Fiona rose from her chair. A sailor, eh? Father would have kittens.

What a charmer, Philip mused, in her little black velvet spencer and powdery blue gown, all that reddish hair a promise of bliss. Wandering around the streets with her valise was certainly a novel way to hawk her goods. Likely she fell down in front of the bank regularly, and some fellow bought her next meal, while she railed about her oppressors. Then she would give her all for a few pounds.

What might be in that valise, he wondered? How did she stay so scrubbed and virginal appearing? He would soon find out, if he had the strength. That might pose a problem.

Philip escorted her out of the inn and into another hackney. He called to the jarvey, "Culross at Park Street."

"Aye, guv."

He climbed in, and she gave him a shove. "You underhanded villain! You were lying all along. Father sent you."

He shoved her back. "Damned tiger cat. I have a house there. What ails you?"

She bristled with suspicion. "It is very close to *my* house."

"Great! Fine! You can bloody walk home when I am done with you."

"What about our bargain?" she cried. "Now you mean to back out? Ha. Men have no honor."

The little wench. "Just shut your mouth."

"Oh!" she squeaked, offended.

"Or I will shut it for you." With that, he pulled her into his arm and kissed her full lips. This turned into a lightning strike to his head. All his muscles shook, he felt terribly weak. She was—He became dazed. Something was going wrong, beware, off course, headed for the rocks. Worse, the vixen melted in his arms like caramel and cast some sort of spell. Philip tried to find a handhold, and it became her. He clung to her, drowning again, freezing, lost. Broke the kiss and gazed into her face.

She resembled a frightened deer, her green eyes big as soup spoons. He was tempted to laugh, or maybe cry.

"I have not been well," he murmured.

"Oh?" she whispered.

"Shipwrecked."

She caught her breath. "I am so sorry."

The hackney stopped before his house. Phillip reached for the door.

"Do be very careful, Philip," she quietly said. "Take your time."

He surely would break into tears. Instead he clambered out, and following, she took his arm. In her other hand was the damnable valise. Philip paid, and they staggered up the walk. God in heaven, he had forgotten her name.

Chapter Two

Fiona, stunned by the kiss, managed to assist him up the brick walk toward the substantial house. On the circular porch, he dropped the brass knocker. A woman in a mob cap and white apron answered and swung the door wide.

"Oh, sir, I am so glad you are safe back," she said, her round face shining. "I finished all the rooms. The Restons have been sent for and will arrive betimes this afternoon with staff. If only we had earlier notice."

"Never mind, Mrs. Graham. This girl, um—"

She piped up. "Fiona. Philip needs to sit down."

"Oh, gracious, yes. Do come to the sitting room and have a chair. May I offer tea?"

"No," he said, strolled to a leather sofa and collapsed onto it.

Fiona put down the valise and rubbed her sore palm.

"I will be in the kitchen, sir." Mrs. Graham left the room.

"Come here," he ordered.

Fiona sidled over to him. "I cannot stay. I must go home."

"Sit down by me."

She perched on the sofa edge. "I have been away from the house so long—that is, I have to get back in with a story to account for the time. I plan to say I went out for a walk, fell down, and you rescued me."

Again that skepticism twinkled in his dark eyes. "Come now, my girl. This flimsy story may impress lads in from the country, but not me. Sit back, relax. In a minute, when I get my breath, we will go upstairs."

"What?" she scoffed. "As if I would. And I doubt you could make the stairs." He talked in riddles, it made her anxious. "If I do not go home promptly, I shall be *ruined*!"

"Folderol. What is in that valise? Are you one of those dominating types, with whips and such torments? Not my style. I trust you can do nicer things, eh? Gentler things?" He reached out and stroked his long fingers down her arm. "Take off that spencer, sweetheart."

Fiona knocked his hand away and jumped up. "You lecherous dog! I am leaving."

He seemed puzzled, the rascal. She stood tall.

"I will come back for the valise later today. If you will, please leave it on the porch. Thank you for the food and everything. I am sorry you are not well."

Fiona dashed for the front door and hastened out it. She would face her father alone. This man Philip was a scamp.

She trotted along Park the few blocks to Green Street and climbed the steps of the corner house, tapped, and Sumpter let her in.

"Miss Fiona! We wondered—what has happened to your head?"

"Oh, I—you will not believe."

Daisy hurried in, her manner troubled. "Where did you go, miss?"

"I went out early for a long walk," Fiona

continued, "to think." She lowered her voice. "Where is my father?"

"His lordship has not come down, miss," Sumpter replied. "He asked only for coffee and the *Times* this morning."

"What happened to your head?" Daisy inquired, leaning closer.

"Well, of all things," Fiona fibbed, "lost in thought, I tripped on a sidewalk crack and fell down. I was quite undone, but a kind man came along and helped me up. I stepped into his house, right down Park Street, and rested for a time. His name was Philip."

They both seemed nonplussed.

"But I am all right now," she added.

"Do you care for breakfast?" Daisy asked.

"No, thank you, the gentleman gave me a cup of tea while I recovered. Then I came home. I will go upstairs for a little."

Fiona climbed the stairs to her room, shut the door, and fell into her chair. The bed had been made and the room picked up. They might know she had lied, but hopefully, would say nothing.

How vexatious. Her plan had not worked at all. She had been a fool to think it would. Now her valise and its precious contents was out of her hands. She must go back as soon as possible and retrieve it.

And ho, Father did not realize she had been gone. She now knew how ruthless he could be, how faithless, to steal her inheritance. She would step all over his deceitful plans and would not be sold off like a brood mare! Fiona did not know what she would try next but set to scheming. There must be a way, and she would find it.

****

Damn the chit, Philip muttered. Fiona, right. He had not asked her last name. The girl was dotty, forget it. No loving today, but he was too tired anyway.

He eyed the brown valise. Dragged it over, clicked the catch, and opened it to survey the contents. No whips or chains. The scent of flowers wafted up to him as he turned over silky garments and muslin stuff. Tiny slippers, satin stays; not garments of the poor. Business must be good. A packet of letters, tied with a red ribbon. Four of them, old, the paper dried out. He unfolded one and read.

Bath. February 12, 1805

Darling Fiona,

I am feeling so much better today. I rest and take the vile waters, famed for their healing powers, but it tastes like coal dust. I have gained a bit of weight, and the cough is subsiding.

I do hope you are attending your school work with regularity. Try to keep your father content, if you can. Meantime, I hope to leave here soon and come home.

Have a good birthday, my love. I hold you in my heart until I can hold you near. Enclosed find a lovely picture of an angel. She reminds me of you.

Hugs and Kisses,

Mama

He turned over a miniature watercolor of a curly-haired cherub. Phillip folded the paper and read the next one.

Bath. February 24, 1805

Darling Fiona,

How good you are to write so often, and your spelling is much improved. Sweet girl, do not blame your father for being cross. Much is on his mind. Do your best, as I know you always try to do. No one could have a better daughter than you, Fiona. Never forget that. I tell everyone here how lovely and talented you are. Remember your piano lessons, and when I come home, we will play that Italian duet you like so much.

Hugs and a dozen kisses.

Mama

Philip read the third.

Bath. March 12, 1805

Darling Fiona,

I am so sorry to fall away from writing, but much has gone on. New doctors to deal with. They are very hopeful my condition can be improved. Do not be troubled by your father being unable to come for me. He is busy, and I am doing just fine. A hired carriage can be easily obtained, and I will ride home in splendor. I cannot wait to see you. We will have such fun.

All my love,

Mama

The man could not be bothered to fetch his ill wife? What kind of...*my unprincipled father*, Fiona had said.

He read the last.

Bath. March 22, 1805

Darling Fiona,

Only one more week. I continue to put up with doctor's orders, but I will be home Thursday next without fail, if I must climb out a window. Fiona, I know how hard this has been for you. Ignore your father when he loses his temper. Leave the room. When I am home again, we will straighten out his lack of

27

manners. Thursday, darling girl. Wait for me.

A hundred kisses,

Mama

Then Philip saw the funeral invitation. A small white card. Severe. No illustration to soften the blow.

Suddenly, at home, April 10, 1805.

The Right Honble. The Viscountess Greathouse, Eleanora Hamilton Seymour, 1775-1805

Wife of The Right Honble. The Viscount Greathouse, Roland Collingwood Seymour.

Mother to The Honble. Fiona Seymour, age nine years.

Burial from Two Twenty Green Street at Park Street to Heavenly Repose Cemetery, London.

2 PM, April 12, 1805. Kindly bring this card.

He was touched. The girl had been truthful. Philip put the letters back under the ribbon and into the valise and closed it, guilty, regretful. He had been about to remove her clothes and see if she was real, but insulted, she had sailed right out the door. What a capital error that would have been! She might have shrieked bloody murder and run for a constable.

And, he acknowledged, that stolen kiss in the hackney had jarred his brain. Coming back for the valise, was she? Maybe. Why should he wait? Green Street was only three blocks away.

Phillip stood, feeling somewhat rested, and walked to the foyer, to find the charlady. "Mrs. Graham? What are the chances of a bath?"

****

Fiona washed her face and hands and idly glanced into the small glass. Horrors! There was a lump on her forehead! She looked like a cyclops. He, that rogue, had not said anything. How bad of him, how dreadful. He was probably laughing at her right now. She dabbed cologne over it, but that stung.

Everything had gone wrong today, everything. Noon already. She smoothed her gown and noticed dirty smudges on the front. Mercy! Falling down in front of the Bank of England was likely equivalent to doing so at court. She changed her gown for another, tussled with the hooks, and left the chamber to go down and have lunch. Hopefully, Father had gone out.

As she ate vegetable soup, Gregg hovering, Fiona thought of the man. Or rather, she thought of the kiss in the hackney. She had endured dampish busses on the cheek by young boys and a few bruising attempts by overeager swains, but nothing like Philip, the sailor.

She studied the effect. His lips captured hers, and it was as if she had been opened up like a book. Exposed, really seen by him and by herself. And it had seemed to herald change. A sudden awareness had occurred, and an elusive…something…had dawned on her. Exactly what, she was unsure. A tickling sensation had emerged in her middle. Fiona liked it and had liked him. His coat smelled of the salty sea. *Take off that spencer*, he had actually said. And she had wanted to. *Sweetheart*, he called her.

Unbelievable. Rather too bad she would not see him again. He would leave the valise on his porch, she would slip it back in the house, and that would be that. She listlessly buttered a roll, and here came her father, newspapers under his arm. He dropped into his chair.

"Am I to have no luncheon? Give me food. Get on with it!" he shouted, casting down the papers.

As he glowered, Daisy hastily set his place at the

mahogany table. Gregg promptly brought his soup and a plate of various cheeses. The maid added fresh rolls in a basket and a selection of fruit.

He fixed his furious eye on Fiona. "Dawdling about, girl? Have you no occupation?"

She opened her mouth to speak, but his attention was taken by Quiggs, peeping around the door.

"What is it, man?" Father yelled. "Have I no peace? Send those damnable letters! Step over to Gleason's and check the numbers. I will not be swindled!"

He turned back to his soup, slurped a spoonful, and pushed his plate away. "Cold! Must I countenance sloppy service?" He stood, shoving his chair back. Daisy and Gregg cowered. Fiona rose, sick of him and his tantrums.

"Do not bully the help, Father. If you want hotter soup, present yourself at the proper hour."

His face went scarlet, all the way down his pudgy neck. "Little bitch," he hissed, "I will soon be shed of you. Just like your mama, weak, shiftless, worth nothing to me."

Fiona became so angry, her vision blurred. She clenched her fists and silently vowed to kill him.

"Cameron will soon have you in his charge," he threatened, "and pay heavily for the dubious privilege. Yes, he will!" He laughed viciously and stormed out of the room.

Daisy, Gregg, and Fiona just stood there, as he stomped up the stairs. Then came a sort of muffled cry and a series of heavy thumps. They hurried to the foyer, and he lay at the foot of the stairs, his face white, his mouth drawn back. Sumpter knelt down, Fiona with him, and the butler spoke.

"My lord, lie still, lie still. Gregg, run for Doctor Calvert. Tell him—"

Fiona touched her father's face. He glanced up at her with a look of bewildered pain. "Worth nothing, worth nothing," he slurred, emitted a throaty gurgle, and his gaze became fixed. They all held a collective breath. Silence seeped into the entire house.

"Never mind, Gregg," Fiona quietly said. "Never mind, it is over."

****

With one thing and another, including falling asleep in his bath, shaving, and dressing without aid, it was nearing three of the clock when Philip walked slowly to Two Twenty Green Street. On the corner of Park, he found a neat white stucco and timber home, three stories, with a well-tended lawn. Most respectable.

There was a lot going on. Two older women waited on the columned porch, large covered baskets in hand. A gentleman was leaving, carrying a black leather bag. A physician? Jesus, not the girl? She had hit her head. Perhaps—Philip dismissed this worry. As the doctor came down the flagstone walk, he spoke. "Sir, may I ask, is there illness here?"

"Eh? No, no, go right on in, young man." The fellow bustled to a waiting barouche, got in, and was driven away.

Philip strolled up the walk as the two women were shown in by a butler. He climbed the steps as the women hurried upstairs.

"Good afternoon. I am Philip Laughton, here to call on Miss Seymour."

The butler, a slight man, faltered.

"Has something untoward happened?" Philip asked. "I trust the lady is well?"

"Yes, sir, she is, but, her father, the viscount—has passed. Just this afternoon. We are in some confusion." The butler dithered, obviously uncertain. "May I take in your card?"

"I have none. I have been long at sea. Not to worry," Philip reassured him. "I am a new friend."

"Yes, sir. One moment." He stepped across the marble tiles to pocket doors.

Philip noted a line of portraits of somber gentlemen, recording the years in their dress and appointments. On the other wall was a lady in a ballgown of the last century, a diamond tiara on her head of rusty curls, her elaborate brocade gown sparkling with jeweled facets.

The butler returned and beckoned. Philip stepped into a room of heavy furniture, dark hangings at the windows. The ample fireplace was cold. There Fiona sat, on a gold embroidered settee, looking very small in a gown of mossy green. The effect made her seem flower-like.

"Mr. Laughton, Miss Fiona."

Her eyes grew to saucers. "Thank you, Sumpter. Please have tea brought, if that is possible."

"Yes, miss."

The butler withdrew, silently closed the doors, and she came to life. "You rascal! What are you doing here?" Then she softly murmured, "Did you bring the valise?"

"No. I wanted to see the lay of the land. What has gone on?"

She fell back against the settee arm. Philip sat down next to her.

"My father—in a temper about something, shouted at us all, then on the way upstairs, he fell all the way back down. And died! Doctor Calvert said it was an apoplexy. I am uncertain what exactly that is, but he is dead all the same."

Philip absorbed this, as her green eyes filled with tears.

"His last words were that I was worthless," she lamented. "Worth nothing, he said, worth nothing."

Philip, affected by her sorrow, put his arm around her shoulders. She leaned against him slightly.

"I am so very sorry," he murmured, inhaling her appealing fragrance. "Are family coming?"

She shook her head. "No, there is no family. Just me. I will manage. Women have come to do the last offices. Sumpter, the butler, has sent word to the…to the carpenter to bring the…"

The girl avoided saying coffin, the poor girl. Philip gave her his handkerchief, and she dabbed her eyes.

"Well," he ventured, feeling protective. "I will help, any way I can."

Now she leaned away. "Why would you?"

He chanced a smile. "We are friends, are we not?"

Puzzled, she said, "Until a moment ago, I did not know your last name. How did you find me?" It quickly dawned on her. Those green eyes blazed. "Hideous man, you read my letters! You poked through my clothing?"

"I did not," he lied. "That is, I read the address. I worried for you, getting back in the house and everything. So, I came to see." He widened his smile. "I shaved. Do I not look nice? I lost flesh in hospital but will gain it back. Am I presentable enough to be your friend?"

She looked him over. "If you can tolerate the lump on my forehead, which you never mentioned."

"I was lost in your green eyes."

She laughed gaily. "Are all sailors so poetically inclined?"

"It varies. What say you? Am I accepted?"

"By all means, sir."

"Philip, please."

"Philip. I am Fiona."

"Yes," he said, his gaze on the rust-red colors of her hair. "Yes, I remembered."

A harried-looking gray-haired maid brought in the tea tray and glanced at him with interest.

"Thank you so much, Daisy. Please take a rest. There is no more to do for a time."

"Yes, miss, I will. Thank you."

Fiona poured out the tea as he watched. Her skin satin, her pretty gown fresh, she was as clean as the dawn. Philip liked her and felt at home in her company. Famished for a fine woman's smell and softness, he might never leave.

Fiona took his attentions in stride. The whole day had been so fantastic, it all fell together and seemed almost ordinary. Father, his final insult still echoing in her ears, would humiliate her no more. He was wrong, and she would prove it. She was free of him, free to make a new life. To find her way in the world, just as she had hoped.

Meanwhile, here was Philip whosit, the sailor. And did he not look charming in his fine clothes? A gold ring with a crest was on the little finger of his left hand. Rather elegant for a seaman. Was that superfine coat borrowed from that grand house? She regarded him closely, with some suspicion, then felt sorry for him. He was tired, poor man, and had not been well.

"Should you not be resting at home, Philip?"

"I had to come."

They gazed at each other. His dark eyes were as brown as amber.

"What made you ill?" she inquired. "What happened?"

"My ship sank," he answered tersely. "I spent some time in icy water."

She knew there was more to the story, but his grim expression closed. "How awful for you. Thank God you survived."

He did not answer, just drank his tea. Fiona's giving nature went out to him.

"Have you eaten? The kitchen is likely in chaos, but if you wait here, I will bring you something."

He smiled again. Mercy, he was handsome.

"I only had our breakfast."

Glad to have something to do for him, she stood. "Have more tea, and I will be right back."

Fiona scurried from the room, along the hall, through the dining room baize door, and down to the kitchens. The portly cook and Irma, a kitchen maid, sat at the deal table as if marooned. They saw her and jumped up.

"Oh, Miss Fiona," Cook mourned, "the master gone, what shall become of us?"

"We will go right on, Mrs. Destin. I have a guest, and he has not eaten. Could you fix a tray, and I will take it back to him?" The women looked glum. "Come now! We are capable women, are we not? We will be fine."

Cook and her helper busied themselves. Fiona, glad to serve her new acquaintance, balanced a tray and retraced her steps to the drawing room. He sat where she had left him. How long his legs were! She placed the tray on an adjacent table.

"Now. There is hot vegetable soup, cheese, and fresh rolls and butter. And a glass of red wine. For strength."

"Wonderful."

He held the large cup, tasted the soup, then ate more. He buttered a roll, and quickly demolished the food.

Fiona was entranced. For all her social gadding, there had been no occasion like this, alone with a sizeable stranger; and in that hackney, he had kissed her like a lover. Then come to see if she was all right. Her heart bumped in her breast.

"Were you in the navy?" she dared to ask.

"In my fashion." He ate the last chunk of cheese.

"What? I should think one is either in or out."

"Very well, I was in. There is a war on, you may have heard."

Rather rude of him. "I only asked, Mr., um, Laughton. For all I know you are a pirate."

"Maybe I am," he hinted.

Fiona found this interesting. He had looked like a pirate in his blue coat, and he did not act like other young men she had met. Now in quality clothing, he could be anyone in the ton. Also, he smelled nice. "Oh, good," she stated. "It must be why you are so appealing."

That grin. "Am I?"

"Certainly. Very dashing and dramatic."

He placed his serviette on the tray. "And you are a very beautiful woman."

"Ohhh," she breathed, surprised.

"Has no one said, Fiona?"

"Mercy, no. I mean, not directly. Not in so many words. Thank you."

They exchanged a long look. Forbidden terms tumbled through her head. Seduction being one of them. Sex followed after that, and she wondered if this talk was a prelude. If he meant to overwhelm her right on this settee. She felt her cheeks warm.

"I have had few such remarkable kisses," he went on as if discussing the weather. "You might have come back for that valise, or you might not have. I was unwilling to let you go. So, here I am. If that suits. Unless you are spoken for?"

She frowned. "My father..." Why not tell him? "The fact of it is," she related, raising her chin, "I was about to be sold off to the highest bidder, to increase his power and influence. My objections were worth nothing, and that was why I ran away. But that is done with. Father is dead, and his arrangements with him."

It was too galling! Furious, she cried, "And I *am* worth something, I know I am. I intend to do good with my life and never marry, except for love. Do you not agree? Otherwise, where is any, um, comfort and affection to be found? Or do only women think that there must be real love?"

He considered this, then replied, "Women, I have observed, tend to put love where there is none. Like a seed they hope will grow. As for men, I only know what I want for myself."

Fiona held her breath.

His gaze was piercing. "Without love, marriage would be a wasteland. I want a dear companion, to share my table and my bed, and whatever troubles come along."

Her tension escaped in a long sigh. "Yes, I agree."

As they chatted, Philip readily saw Fiona's innocence and vulnerability. Now she was all on her own, and he felt the urge to take care of her. Just a girl, really. She needed protection. He would linger for a time and perhaps provide a helping hand. The journey from Dover to London had been arduous enough. His business in town was incomplete, and getting home had come to seem daunting. He could recover himself a little here as well as there, and all the other tasks could wait. *Sorry, Uncle,* he apologized. *I will get there, I promise.*

A tap at the door. "Come," she called.

The butler peered in. "Beg pardon, Miss Fiona. All the preliminaries are complete. The viscount is at rest in the library. Mr. Frisk has a few matters he wishes you to approve."

She sat erect and folded her small hands. "Send him along, Sumpter, if you will."

"Yes, miss."

Philip made to stand.

She touched his sleeve. "No, Philip, just stay there and rest. I know what he wants."

A robust, red-faced fellow entered, looking more like a greengrocer than an undertaker.

"Miss Seymour," he oozed, "my deepest

condolences. Viscount Greathouse was the epitome of—"

"Yes, Mr. Frisk, he certainly was. I assume you want the wording for the funeral card?"

"Ah, yes, if you would. Now, there are several choices, such as…" He took cards from a pocket and displayed them. "Flower bouquets are popular, or one of a selection of angels?"

"No. A plain card, white."

He whipped out a stub of pencil and licked it, holding aloft a piece of paper.

She dictated. " 'Suddenly, at home, The Right Honorable The Viscount Greathouse, Roland Collingwood Seymour, 1759-1815.' When may the burial be scheduled?"

"Within three days, ma'am. Given the warm weather."

"Then day after tomorrow, in the early afternoon. Burial from this address to Heavenly Repose Cemetery, London. When you have it, add that time and date. Quiggs will provide a list of whom the cards should go to. There will not be many."

"Shall family names be added?" Frisk inquired, his pencil poised. "Or your own, perhaps?"

"No, thank you, Mr. Frisk. There is no family to inform. That will do. Please fill the library with flowers promptly. I trust you will see to the rest of what is required?"

"Yes, ma'am. Every little thing has been seen to. Flowers will arrive before evening; I will attend to that myself." The paper went into his pocket. "Well, then. Again, my sympathy. If there is nothing else, I bid you good day."

"Good day."

Frisk backed out and was gone.

Philip watched all this transpire. The card sounded as chill as the man had been toward her mother. Fiona would not even associate herself with him. What a legacy he had left.

She turned to him. "No doubt you think me heartless."

"No, my dear. I think you heartsore."

"He stole my inheritance!" she stated. "Insulted and belittled me for years. No one will ever do that again." Her expression softened. "I am so glad you were here, Philip. It has made the moment easier. Thank you."

He was delighted. "I will stay in town for the present, Fiona, and offer you my aid. Anything you need done, I will endeavor to handle."

Her green eyes widened. "Oh, could you? Just while you rest? Or must you report for duty?"

"No, I have medical leave. Three months off was ordered."

He saw her relief. She smiled, and Philip thought her lovelier than ever. A hubbub in the foyer and a booming voice drew her attention.

"Oh, no," she whispered, "I forgot about *him*."

A commotion at the doors. An exclamation, a scuffle, and in hastened a rather fat, short fellow, full of his own importance. His pompous appearance was so comical, Philip hid a smile.

"Fiona, my dear," he fairly yelled, rushing to her. "Sumpter informed me. What a tragedy! I am here to lend you my services. Fear not, I will take care of everything."

His watery gaze shifted to him. Philip slowly rose from the settee and towered over him.

"Who the devil is this?" the donkey demanded to know.

Fiona stood as well. "You can have no further concern with this house or with me, Lord Cameron. And you need know nothing of my friends. My father will be buried day after tomorrow. It has been thoroughly seen to, and your attendance will not be required."

Cameron paid her no mind. "So!" he accused in a loud voice. "This is the other man, eh? A reprobate, out to take advantage of an innocent! A nobody, an upstart commoner. Entirely unworthy of—"

Philip held his temper, to let it play out.

"Please go," Fiona ordered. "Like my father, you are abusive and demanding. I wish never to see you again."

Affronted, his pudgy face turned dark. "You will belong to me, Fiona," he jeered through gritted teeth. "The contract has been signed."

"Not by me, sir. By a man now dead."

The dolt scowled, creasing his broad forehead into ruts. "Little fool," he snarled, "how do you think I got his consent? Eh? Eh? I will tell you."

The man moved closer to Fiona. Philip went on guard.

"I own you!" Cameron sneered. "I own everything. This house, the property, and all it contains. And, haughty miss, the very clothing you stand in. I saw you coldly dismiss and discourage suitors. I knew you would not consent to marry me, stubborn, willful girl, so I made sure you must. I hold your father's substantial debts. All of them."

Fiona shook with indignation, and Philip stepped to the man. "Get out of this house."

"What?" he screeched. "You dare to address me? Do you know who I am? I can defeat you, I can—"

He grabbed the man by his coat collar, lugged him bodily to the doors and into the foyer, his boots dragging. The obliging butler opened the front door. Philip tossed the beggar out, and Sumpter threw his hat and stick after him. Cameron, much disheveled, picked himself up, slammed on his hat, and gestured angrily.

"I will have her," he bellowed, "or she will be penniless. I will take everything. All of it! Everything!"

Philip turned away, and Sumpter closed the door. Fiona stood at the drawing room doors, her face amazed.

"Let us sit down, Fiona." He gently took her arm and they returned to the settee.

"Cameron is an oaf," she declared. "My father—"

"Signed you away?"

"Yes, he did. And if he owns all—but then, maybe he lied, seeking an advantage."

"If I am correct, death renders most contracts null and void. He was likely bluffing."

Her expression clouded. "He means me to marry him or starve? Can you imagine? I will kill myself first, and I told him so."

"Cannot have that, dear girl."

"Then, what shall I do?"

"Kiss me."

She laughed uncertainly.

Philip got an arm around her and drew her closer. "You will not marry that blockhead."

"What can be done against him?" she whispered.

"Plenty."

And he kissed her soft lips.

Fiona lost any sense of reality. Kissing Philip filled her head with clouds of pleasure, and everything else fell away. He kissed her cheek and her ear, and thrilled, she nestled in his arms. Rather strong arms for a sick man, she mused. At one point, Cameron's boots had almost left the floor.

"Not to worry, Fiona," he murmured in her ear, raising gooseflesh. "Tomorrow I will see my man of business and straighten these matters out."

Mystified, she asked, "You have a man of business?"

"I do."

She eased away. What sort of person was this? "Philip," she began.

"I have, and am," he said, "many things we have not had sufficient time to discuss. Can you trust me?"

She waved her hand. "Oh, certainly, after rescuing me on the cold sidewalk and casting my tormentor into the dust. Tomorrow Cameron will come with *his* man of business, and I will go out that same door."

"All will be resolved. He cannot force your agreement, and we will not be influenced by his ire. Odd. What kind of man thinks to buy a wife?"

"A weird one. Cameron set his fixed attention on me since Christmas. I knew it but avoided him, as I have avoided others I did not care for. He took other measures and, like a table, found me for sale." Her green eyes turned cold as she went on. "I have no man of business or anything else. Father ran our affairs. I was nobody, just a pawn to be dressed up and shown off to catch a rich man. How stupid of me to never understand my true position."

Philip just sat there quietly, his arm around her. Fiona had the trained impulse to object to such familiarity, but why? The old rules had fallen away since he had gotten her into that hackney. And in his warm arms, she felt safe.

She touched his coat. "I think you have not told me important things, Philip."

He put his fingers into her hair. Her scalp tingled.

"No, but I will. I need permission to speak."

"Permission?" she asked, gazing into his mellow brown eyes.

"From the navy. Then I will tell you all."

"You are not a pirate?" she joked.

"Sadly, no. I will seek that approval tomorrow."

Her sympathy doubled. "Oh, you are too tired to do all that. It can wait. You need rest."

"I also need exercise," he answered. "I have been idle too long. I liked kissing you, Fiona. It was healthful and renewed my strength."

She giggled. He was so far out of her orbit, she could say what she liked. "Far be it from me to withhold such a tonic. It makes me feel better, too. Oh, Philip. I confess I have never indulged in kissing. I never met anyone I wanted to kiss. Like that. Like you."

"I never would have guessed. You seem expert."

He ran his thumb over her lower lip, startling her.

"Your freshness and beauty are very alluring, Fiona. I can see why you were pursued by others, raising Cameron's lust."

"More like his greedy possession. I rather think lust

is frowned on in the ton."

"Not so, my friend. Sex runs like an underground river under all the ton does, says, and requires. The rigid, stodgy rules and requirements are forgotten hourly. It is entirely a social façade, run by the doyens, meant to shut out those who will not obey, and rein in all who will. It is a power game."

Fiona absorbed this. "Father pushed me to be a part of it. I am a viscount's daughter and must...well, conform. He said—" Fiona pushed the thought aside. "What do I care what he said? I mean to go my own way, but do not yet know what that is." It made her nervous. "I have no society but the ton. I would have no friends without them."

"You could have me," he suggested. "Exclusively."

It made her happy to think so, and she smiled. "How nice you are, Philip."

He curled a tendril of her hair around his long finger. "Is that why you kiss me so sweetly?"

Fiona loved this highly unusual intimacy. "I kiss you because I want to. Because you are a very diverting and dangerous man."

Philip grinned. "Dangerous, am I?"

"Yes, decidedly. You rapidly overwhelmed Cameron, and it appears I am helpless before you. I must beg for mercy, sir."

"Do not bother," he said, holding her closer. "I have no mercy."

And he kissed her again, longer, deeper than before. It lit a small blaze in Fiona's center, just below her heart. Perhaps even a little lower than that.

Chapter Three

Unwillingly, Philip took his leave.

Fiona fussed over him endearingly. "Let me have the carriage brought around."

It made him smile. "It is only three blocks. I need the walk; it gets my lungs working."

Her green eyes misted. "Please take care. I wish very much that you should be well."

He held her for another tender kiss. "I will see about my obligations and be back tomorrow."

"I will wait."

They rose, Fiona took his arm, and they strolled to the doors. She stopped, her expression tense, and clasped her hands together. "Philip, I am fearful."

"Say not."

"This day has been such an upheaval. I have done unimaginable things."

"Kissing me, you mean?" he teased.

"Yessss, and ordering Cameron out, and—"

He cupped her chin in his hand. "You are up to it all, my girl. You are brave, strong, and know your own mind. Right there, you are ahead of the mob. And I will deal with the officious Cameron."

She gulped. "You will have him beaten?"

"God, no. I can best him with legal means. If it comes to that."

They stepped into the foyer, the butler on duty.

"If I may take the liberty to speak for you, Fiona?" Philip asked.

"Please."

"Sumpter," he said, "you have seen what a disgusting pest Lord Cameron is. I suggest he not be admitted to further threaten and harass the household. I will return tomorrow, I hope with some answers to guide us."

The slender butler nodded, his expression sober. "Certainly, sir. The man shall not enter."

"Excellent." Philip took Fiona's small hand. A wave of affectionate concern welled in his chest. It was easy to care about what happened to her. "Until then, my dear." He bent, kissed her cheek, and walked out the door, sorry to leave her company.

Philip managed the three blocks home better than earlier. After all, he had done nothing but sit with Fiona and kiss her pretty lips. A fine form of rest. She picked up all his spirits. He breathed deeply. No cough, no congestion.

He arrived to find the welcome presence of the Restons. The male of the pair, a cautious, eternally wary person, opened the door and, after seeing Philip was alone, beamed. "My lord, how grand. To find you home again is a joy."

He stepped inside. "Good to see you, Reston."

"We received your message from the hospital. It near knocked us over, but at least you had not been shot to pieces or blown apart."

Mrs. Reston hurried into the room, a smiling, jolly presence in contrast. "Hush now, Mister, with your gruesome stories. My lord, you look a picture. A mite thin, but we can fatten you up again." She leaned closer, and Philip smelled furniture polish. "Was it the French that got you?"

"The French or their friends, Missus. I am off duty for a time and mean to rest up."

"That you shall, sir. Your rooms are all ready. A letter was delivered for you, and I put it in the study."

"Well and good."

"Dinner will be at six, my lord. Kitchen maids and Cook Maud are installed."

"Thank you, Missus. I will be in the study until then."

Down the hall, he entered the study and turned the lock. He sat down in his chair, turned the lamp higher, broke the seal on the letter, and read.

Congratulations, you sea dog.

Pears Tobacconist, 214 Jermyn Street. Ask for a Turkish blend, 2+2.

M.

Philip put the letter into the fire and watched it burn. Not done with him yet, eh? Another little thing needed doing, now he was on his feet again. Well, he would report in and extricate himself from this latest intrigue. His responsibilities had increased; he had other obligations and people who depended on him. Bloody all of it weighed on him.

He consoled himself with recollections of the afternoon with Fiona. He had not met anyone so affectionate, so innocent. Her kisses, her female scent, and her saucy taking on of the world enchanted him. She was a thousand miles from war and death, bearing sweetness and beauty. Philip had once thought beauty was all that mattered, before he sailed away with a cargo of secrets. Years before. Could he ever regain that serenity, that ease?

****

Fiona drifted back to the drawing room, alternating between effervescence regarding Philip Laughton and a nagging worry that her world was fast crumbling. The season in full swing, a stack of invitations were on her dressing table. All her friends might be wondering where she had gone. Did she really care? Did they? High time she moved on. Now Father would not be poking her with a stick to succeed. Young girls were led like lambs to slaughter, she grieved.

Well, that was over. The ton galas celebrated themselves, and it had often been difficult for her just getting though an evening. Her attendance was required; her smiles and her dances were demanded. To fit in, to be one of them, to snag wealthy suitors. Now there was only herself. It gave her a terrible sense of isolation to know so little of life. To be alone in the world.

Fiona ate a tasty dinner, Gregg and Daisy quiet.

"I do not want anyone to worry," she declared. "Your places here are safe. I could not get on without you."

"Truly, Miss Fiona?" Daisy whispered.

"Absolutely. We are all in this together and will survive. My new friend, Mr. Laughton, is clever and has resources. He has vowed to help, including fending off nasty Lord Cameron."

"Cheers, miss," Gregg happily said.

Dessert was a mocha mousse, and Fiona licked her spoon, thinking of Philip's dark eyes and soft mouth. She thanked the servants, and in the hall, turned toward the library. The paneled door was closed. A rolled rug lay against the threshold. Fiona resolutely pushed it away and went in. The windows thrown wide, the room was chill. There he lay, on the long, narrow table where formerly had lain folders of papers. The open coffin, the lid moved aside for viewing, made him appear shorter. His hair had been combed back; his pale face lacked color.

The promised flowers were banked around the table. The pungent mums, carnations, and lilies suffused the area with melancholy odors.

Fiona regarded him. "He is dead," she whispered to herself, trying to make it actual. Trying to care, but she did not. He would never speak again or chide her for her failures. Demean her, steal from her, trade her for riches. Or to settle his debts; how tawdry. Had he stolen her money to pay his creditors, and possibly Cameron? She turned away. It did not matter now. If she had bound herself to a man she did not want, creating misery for her entire life, her father would not have cared. Now, neither did she.

Unexpectedly, tears brimmed her eyes and ran hotly down her cheeks. Why, why, she longed to cry out, why did you never love me? Her plea silent, no answer came. Fiona wiped her tears away and left the library. She pushed the rug against the door, strolled to the stairs, and up.

Tomorrow, she would begin again. Do what must be done. Stay hopeful. And in the afternoon, Philip would come back. This thought raised her mood, and smiling, she went to her room.

****

Tuesday

Pears Tobacconist was painted a weathered green.

The dingy shop listed somewhat to starboard on a Jermyn Street corner. Philip walked slowly by, went once around the block, and entered. A tinny bell over the door sounded as he did so. No other customers.

A shabbily dressed fellow looked up from his newssheet. "Mornin' to ye, sor," he muttered.

Philip longingly eyed a carton of skinny Jamaican cheroots he must not smoke. "Morning. I am interested in your Turkish blend. A 2+2 was recommended."

The fellow responded, "Aye, we got in fresh just yesterday. I have a measure already packed." He reached below the counter and brought up a small, brown leather pouch.

"Very good," Philip said. "What is the charge?"

"Naught. Try it out, sor. You will be pleased. Come back any time for more."

Philip pocketed the pouch. "Thank you." He turned and strolled out. Again, he circled the block in the other direction, glancing in shop windows, catching the reflections of those passing, but he was not followed.

He hailed a hackney, rode to St. James Park, and entered the large building of offices opposite. Philip went through an exit at the far side of the lobby, turned down a hallway, and climbed a short flight of steps. He opened an unmarked door and went in. The outer office was empty, as always. He knocked at a second door.

A deep voice said, "It is open."

Philip walked in to face the man known as Malrose, seated behind a cluttered wood desk. The well-tailored fellow, his left hand badly maimed, grinned, his long face seamed and sardonic. "So, Colbourne. Sit. I trust you are in good health?"

"Mending." He took the leather pouch from his

pocket and placed it on the desk.

"Excellent." Malrose quickly opened it, took out an oilskin packet, and carefully unwrapped it. Within its layers, he extracted a number of small, stiff, parchment papers and glanced over them.

Philip regarded them impassively.

"I commend you, Colbourne."

"Officially, as of yesterday, I assumed my uncle's title."

"Hmm. Keep it quiet. It will not reach the ears of the public for days yet. I have a vital task for you, now you are well."

"*Well*, am I?" Philip's anger surged. "It cost me dearly to put those documents on your desk, Malrose. Weeks in the hospital, for one, my entire crew, my ship. I am done with you." He stood. "I have three months leave, and I am taking it."

Malrose gestured with his good hand. "Sit down, sit down. One last mission, and only you can fulfill it. Please, hear me out."

Philip wearily sat again. "Only me? I have nothing left to give. I am worn out, useless."

"No, you are not. You are precisely the man for this."

Malrose waited for his full attention. Despite himself, Philip listened.

"We have learned that traitors are in our midst. Titled men with financial interests in France are betraying the realm. You can help identify them."

Surprised, he asked, "Englishmen?"

Malrose nodded. "Members of the ton, possibly known to you. Possibly approachable."

"I have not been in London for more than two

years," Philip countered.

"That is what makes it perfect. You will present yourself as an ill man, unable to serve, and highly discontent with the war. You have come up from Hampshire to see your medical people. Two men have now been positively linked to the plot. One is Lord Meacham, and the second is Lord Harley."

Philip nodded. "I met them some years ago, when they were fashionable, and I was young."

"Lastly, of greatest importance, we seek a third. The money man, as yet unidentified. He makes no open contact with the other two, but we know he is passing information and funds to the French."

"My God, Malrose," he complained. "I am not fitted for such work. I want nothing to do with this."

Malrose leaned back in his chair. "No? The bastards we seek had you blown out of the water."

Philip gripped the chair arms. "The hell you say!"

"These maps are battle plans," Malrose intoned, a finger on the parchments, "drawn in Napoleon's hand. They are a run-up to the invasion of England."

Shocked, Philip said nothing.

"The spy who handed you the oilskin packet had his throat slashed. That French cutter followed your wake, circled around, and fired on you."

"Christ!"

"Take revenge, sir. Expose these traitors. With your connections, I know you can." He took cards from a drawer. "Here are three invitations to prestigious social gatherings this week. The two men mentioned are likely to attend one or another event. The object will be to observe them carefully. This unknown third man will possibly contact one or both of the other two, under cover of a crowded social event, and we will know his identity."

Philip again did not speak.

"Time is precious, Colbourne. French troops are being organized as we speak. These maps are the proof. We must find this turncoat and cut off the supply of money and information. We cannot risk invasion."

He mused over this. "You think the French are convinced the maps were lost?"

"Yes. The cutter captain reported he left the *Calliope* unmanned, on fire, and sinking. But you made it, and your eventual Dover handoff was successful. That packet did some roundabout traveling to arrive at Pears."

Philip did not like it. "Your plan sounds damn sketchy, Malrose."

"It is. That is why I depend on you. You are a cool operator, and I know what you can do. Go right on as the reclusive Colbourne. It is a fine disguise."

"I will give it one week," Philip grumbled, standing.

"I accept with the king's thanks."

"How bloody lofty, Malrose." He scooped up the invitations. "These three, no more. And I will cruise White's. I may learn things there."

Malrose slowly stood, his other injuries, souvenirs of Egypt, evident in his stance. "I rely on you with confidence, Colbourne."

"An honor, I am sure. I will be in touch. You use the same address?"

"Yes. Good luck."

Philip exited the building, attracting no undue attention. He caught another hackney and proceeded to the Inns of Court and climbed a flight of stairs, not wheezing, breathing deeply. He stopped at the door marked Kelton and March, Barristers and Solicitors, turned the knob, and stepped inside.

Peebles rose from his desk, took one look, and smiled broadly. "My Lord Colbourne! How fine to see you again."

"How are you, Peebles?"

"Tiptop, sir. Mr. Kelton is in. Mr. March is unavailable. May I announce you?"

Mysterious Mr. March was never available. "Please."

A few moments and a jovial Kelton, his frizzled blond hair in disarray, looked around the door. "Colbourne, come in, come in!"

Philip sauntered in, as Kelton marveled to see him. "I worried! I send letters, and the same cryptic answer comes back. Lord Colbourne is traveling, Lord Colbourne is traveling."

"Well, it was one thing and another. I have business in London and wanted to stop by."

"Excellent, sir. Take a chair. Have a cigar? Brandy?"

Damn those cigars. "A glass would be welcome."

Kelton poured, handed off the glass, and resumed his seat behind a bare cherrywood desk.

"As well," Philip went on, "I have a question."

"Ask away."

"A young lady friend finds herself in a situation. Her overbearing father signed a marriage contract, without her consent, to a man she despises. Then, the father abruptly died. The so-called fiancé threatens to force her to obey the terms or face poverty, since he claims to hold the late father's considerable debts."

"Ah. That amounts to coercion and is illegal. Contracts signed, however, are signed. If broken, the lady can be sued for breach of promise. Quite ridiculous to do so, however. I would need to go over the document." Kelton smiled, his manner cheeky. "Or, if you, sir, are the friend of said friend, he could come after you for alienation of affections. In short, he could create a stir."

Philip downed his brandy. "Who honors the promise of a dead man? And I have alienated nothing from anyone. I only met her recently. However, she hates him and threatens to kill herself rather than marry him. Unlikely, but you can see what a bind this is for the lady."

Kelton pulled his chin. "Hmmm. I would depend on the forces of the ton. Of which, I allow these two are members?"

"Yes."

"Drop a word in the right places, Colbourne. Let gossip take its toll. My lady love assures me the ton moves on wheels of rumor and inuendo. The fellow will likely shrink from being publicly rejected by his intended victim. He will be painted as a fool if his threats become known. Yes, I would see to that public revelation."

"These debts of the father he holds. Can he take her property and possessions?"

"Not unless he goes to court. And it would take an extended time to find he cannot collect from a dead man or his heirs unless contractually specified. Most unlikely of the parties to have added such a clause. Yet another blot on his name to hound a lady obviously in mourning."

"Good, Kelton, good. I will relay these judgements. If it progresses against her, I will request you take the case. If you would."

"Of course. A meaty little problem to solve. Just for drill, might I know his name?"

"He is the Earl of Cameron."

Kelton nodded sagely. "Ho, ho! A havey-cavey fellow, as my father used to say."

"Oh?"

"Speculations regarding him have circulated. Shady financial dealings; questionable friends among those who disapprove of the lingering war."

Philip came to attention. "Do such groups exist openly, Kelton?"

"They simmer, here and there, just below the surface. One can sometimes detect the rancid odor."

"Jesus," Philip murmured. "Do you know everything that goes on?"

The solicitor preened, smoothing back his unruly hair. "Nearly. And every day, I learn more."

They laughed, Philip rose, and Kelton saw him to the door.

"Glad to see you, Colbourne. Pray, when I send letters, tell your people to stop saying the same thing."

"I would, Kelton, but I am traveling."

Kelton grimaced good-naturedly. Philip said goodbye to Peebles and left the office.

****

Fiona woke late and hurriedly washed and dressed. The knowledge of her father lying dead in the library below cast a pall over the sunny spring day, but she pressed on. At breakfast, Gregg and Daisy were subdued, befitting the nearby presence of a corpse.

"Things are going well in the kitchens, Gregg?" she inquired, to make conversation.

"Oh, yes, miss. We have all recovered ourselves from the passing. Cook particularly." He assumed a contemplative air. "The master will know no more pain."

And neither will we, she thought. "I cannot say he had any pain, but he will suffer none in the future."

Daisy rolled her eyes piously, but Fiona knew better. Her father had been an iron collar around all their necks. She drank her coffee, trying not to visualize his ghost walking through the wall to haunt her.

Breakfast over, Fiona was at loose ends. She returned to her room and went through her gowns. There was no need to change from her morning gown, she had nowhere to go. She took the seventeen shillings, eight pence from her reticule and returned them to the tin box under the shelf. Then she considered she might need some money. Father had paid for everything, what could she do if someone presented a bill? Who was going to—of course! Quiggs would pay everyone! Nevertheless, she took out five shillings and dropped them in her reticule. She replaced the key in her drawer and sat down feeling scattered and uncertain.

Quiggs would pay if there were funds to do so. And someone had to pay him. And where was he? Daisy arrived to tidy the room.

"Ah, Daisy, has Quiggs come today?"

"No, miss," she answered, making the bed. "He came back yesterday afternoon." She fluffed the pillows. "He was right shocked, bowled over to learn what had happened to the master. Denied use of the library, he allowed he would come back around noon today to see if anything was required. That is what he said." Daisy shook the comforter with a snap.

"Very good," Fiona replied. Quiggs would have answers.

Daisy gathered items to be laundered and left the room. Fiona went through her new invitations. A musicale, a lecture on the South Seas, a dinner party. She put them aside. The most ornate card, propped against the glass for days, announced a ball tonight at the Featherstones', to announce their daughter Anna's engagement. Anna was an old school friend from Miss Peabody's. Fiona did not know her betrothed but had looked forward to seeing Anna again and wishing her well.

And her new gown of peach silk, set aside for the occasion, was beyond lovely. Now she could not go. Perhaps she would never be invited anywhere again, she considered sadly. Cameron would trample her reputation. No telling what he might say if she were not there to refute it.

Fiona began to feel quite oppressed. The room seemed to close in on her. She jumped up, hurried out and down the hall. Darted down the stairs, past the library door, and out the back doors to her garden plot. All was well there, colorful and reassuring. Growing and blooming symbols of hope. She put on a battered straw hat and an old leather glove and set to pulling small weeds and deadheading the mixed flowers.

Gradually, her mind settled. Among the birdsong and beneath the gentle sun, her confidence seeped back in. She could make it. Whatever happened, she would be all right. If the ton did not want her, why care? The world was wide, Fiona told herself, glad, at least for the moment, to believe it.

****

Philip bumped over the cobbles; his hackney headed to Park and Green Streets. Blast Malrose for talking him into another assignment, but the man could not be denied. A hero of the Battle of the Nile, he had paid a stark price early on in the conflict.

He remembered the two titled men mentioned. He had been down from Oxford for Christmas holidays, in London to carouse with his friends. To celebrate, to stretch youthful wings cramped by scholarly restrictions. They had made the rounds of the theaters and the full-bosomed opera dancers. One evening, they journeyed to the notorious gambling hell of Mrs. Black. There, Philip had been introduced to Meacham, when the man joined a loo table. In a short time, Harley, somewhat foxed, his shirtfront askew, had moseyed over to the game.

"Nasty lil cunt stole my pocketbook," Harley had raucously divulged.

Meacham, a foppish, overdressed man, cynically laughed. "More the fool you, pitiable sod," he had replied.

Philip lost ten pounds, his set limit, considered the low company beneath him, and quit the table. He and his friends left the place, discussing how common and gaudy it had seemed.

How innocent he had been, how above it all, his head full of beguiling language. In the years that followed, Philip had encountered men rougher and more offensive than he could have imagined then. He had learned to make his way among them but had not, however, forgotten the pair of ruffians. A disgrace to their rank then, their sins had obviously multiplied.

The hackney stopped before the Seymour house, and Philip stepped down. He paid the jarvey, strode up the flagstone walk, and on the porch, dropped the brass knocker with a thump.

Sumpter opened it a crack, then farther, his expression relieved. "Mr. Laughton, good day, sir. Do step in."

"Has Cameron come around?" he asked, handing off his hat.

"Not as yet, sir. I am on guard. He will not enter this house."

"Good man, Sumpter. Is Miss Fiona about?"

"Yes, sir, in her garden. This way."

Philip followed the butler down the hall to the back doors.

"Just there, sir. Miss Fiona takes great solace in her flowers."

"Thank you, Sumpter."

"Yes, sir."

Sumpter went away, and Philip regarded Fiona as she toiled among the plants. Delectable in a sprigged blue muslin gown, her hands busily pulled small weeds, her pretty face relaxed. His heart moved right over; he felt it.

Had he lost his senses? He only met her yesterday but had hurried back to see her again, as though—The little vixen had put the hex on him. He had enjoyed women from everywhere yet stood there in a trance, famished for her company. He had no time for this. Duty was on his back; new and old obligations nagged him. Plus Malrose and all that. He opened the door and went out into the sunshine, longing to be with her, and mildly annoyed to feel that way.

She glanced up and smiled brilliantly. Philip was instantly charmed.

"Greetings," she called.

"Fiona."

She came toward him, dirt on her nose, wearing a tattered straw hat and a large leather glove.

"You always find me in disarray," she said, still smiling. "But the mark on my forehead is gone. See?"

"A vast improvement. Your nose is dusty."

"Oh, dear, I put on this glove, and then my nose itched."

"Wait," he said, and brushed the dirt away, then he bent and kissed her lips.

Her cheeks turned rosy, as she put the hat and glove on a bench. "I-I cannot believe we have, um, gotten on such friendly terms in only one day," she shyly said, her voice sincere. "Perhaps I should say that I have very little experience with men and such? Lest you should think me fast."

"Not likely, my dear. And what do you think?"

She considered this with a small frown. "That, as I have been warned, it can be deceptively easy to fall into the high weeds."

He had to laugh. "I can truthfully say, Fiona, that I have waited the better part of today to kiss you again."

"But Philip, I—"

"Enough of your objections, girl. I know the things you have been told. I also know I like to kiss you, and you like to be kissed, so let us just leave all those rules outside in the rain."

"It is not raining."

"In that other world it is, but not here."

She searched his face, her green eyes gold in the sunshine.

"Fiona, I am an honorable man, as men go. All of us are knaves, but I solemnly promise never to offend you in any way. Besides frequent kissing, that is. If that counts."

"Thank you. What should I promise?"

"To continue to be yourself, a most delightful lady. And perhaps give me a bite of lunch?"

"Oh, yes. I am hungry, too."

He reached for her hand, and smiling, she took his. Right away, Philip felt better about everything, and they walked inside.

****

Philip sat in her father's chair at the head of the table. Fiona admired him as Daisy, her expression interested, placed bowls of lentil soup before them. She added a plate of cold ham slices, the mustard pot, yeast rolls, butter, and a dish of seasoned beans. Gregg, his face inscrutable, filled glasses with wine.

They began to eat, Fiona fascinated by Philip Laughton. He had excellent table manners. Today, he wore a coat of pale gray superfine, a snowy cravat, and a linen shirt with pearl buttons. He was elegant in every instance. His hand was slightly calloused when he took hers. His black hair had grown long, reaching his collar, but it distinguished him. Those dark eyes seemed to look right through her, which was disconcerting.

The bowls were removed, as Fiona tried to really see him. What in the world was he doing here? Could the fine clothes he wore so casually be his? A sailor surely could not afford such. Did that house belong to him? Why, when he arrived, had he never eaten? Were his pockets empty? At the inn, he had readily spent that sixpence.

Her heart shrank with doubt. What did he want? He knew she had no ready money. She had nothing to offer but her person, which he seemed fond of kissing. But he had been gentlemanly, except for requesting she remove her spencer. What would he have done if she had?

"Eat your lunch," Philip softly said, his deep voice making vibrations in her bones, "and stop worrying."

"Well, it is not worry, exactly. I am trying to place you. Somewhere that fits."

He just smiled and put mustard on his plate, cut into the ham, and chewed.

"My world is rather small, you see," Fiona went on, trying to explain. "The same sort of people move in it. And I know them."

"You found the men dull."

She leaned forward. "Pardon?"

"They bored you. Why else would you turn them all down? You avoided them, you said."

"It was just that Father...so they—oh, I do not know." Fiona longed to escape this scrutiny.

His smile became arrogant. "*I* do not bore you."

"What male crust!" she objected.

He swallowed his wine. "You delight me, Fiona. I cannot stay away."

She glanced at his empty plate. "I begin to think you get hungry and come over for refreshments."

"You give them to me in abundance. A fine lunch, just the thing. My compliments to the cook, Gregg."

The footman jumped to be addressed. "Oh, yes, sir, thank you, sir."

Direct her servants, would he? Fiona steamed for unknown reasons as Daisy cleared dishes and Gregg brought in the sweet.

Philip fairly breathed in the pound cake and strawberries before she could raise her fork. Truth tell, she had never eaten with such a large man. Her father had eaten lightly, conscious of his tendency to gain flesh. Fiona never thought about it.

Just coming here, Philip disarranged everything. How annoying. Held what she did, how she thought, up to view. Maybe she was adjusting to her father's death, or maybe it was time for this review. Maybe she should leave, run right down the street, and never come back.

"Delicious," Philip said dabbing his lips, those tempting lips, with his serviette.

"Would you like coffee?" she asked.

"In the drawing room, please? I have things to tell you."

Every iota of her being came to attention. "Do you?"

"Oh, yes. Lots of things."

Fiona had to catch an extra breath. "Would you please see to that, Gregg?"

"Yes, miss. Right away."

Philip rose and drew out her chair. Doing so, he breathed on her neck. Fiona's entire left side prickled. She stood, and fully in command, he firmly took her arm. My God, she thought, I have been bodily captured by a buccaneer.

Chapter Four

Philip and Fiona sat close together on a tapestry sofa before the fire. The blaze cheered the gloomy room considerably. The girl had an edge of wariness in her expression and needed encouragement.

"I spoke to my man of business this morning, Fiona."

Her eyes lit up.

"I mentioned your problem with Cameron. He advised that it was unlikely the earl could legally take your possessions. It would involve a court battle and take forever. Likely a judge would deem it impossible for him to collect debts from a dead man. Meanwhile, what you have is yours to enjoy."

"As simple as that?" she queried. "Would he create a scandal?"

"He could try, but it would put him in a very poor light to pursue the defunct contract and a woman who does not want him."

"Yessss. I never heard of such a thing."

"The other piece of advice was to drop a few hints to the ton that he was an unsuitable nuisance and you would croak before considering him. Then gossip may take care of the insect."

"But I cannot go out to see anyone. I am in mourning."

"Hmm. Who outside this house knows of the

death?" he asked.

"The cards have yet to be approved when Frisk returns. So far, only Cameron. Father's secretary, Quiggs, knows, too, and is coming back today. I intend to ask him what my finances are. I dearly hope I am not destitute."

"Not to worry, Fiona."

She nibbled her lower lip, raising Philip's temperature.

"There is nothing to sell," she murmured. "I have a necklace from my mother, very fine matched pearls. I could not part with them. I will go hungry before I resort to a pawnshop."

"I agree."

"The servants, however, depend on their pay. Various household bills will fall due. I must ask Quiggs what the situation is."

"I will advance you whatever is needed."

She did not seem to hear him. "I never thought of it. I was so foolish. Food, firewood, coal, and all of it. I just had my head in a bag. It makes me ashamed."

He touched her silken, rusty hair with a fingertip. "Of what?"

"Not paying attention! Never knowing where I stood. I knew Father wanted me to marry a titled, rich man. I just kept putting it off. He craved distinction, and I was the mantrap to get it for him."

"But you did not oblige."

"No. I could not exhibit myself in that way, and that made him angry, so he scolded and humiliated me. I did not want any of it, Philip. I knew a decision was coming and did nothing, imagining I had time."

"What is your age, Fiona?"

"I was nineteen in February."

He nodded. "Yes, your mother mentioned the date."

She was so shocked, her mouth fell open. Then she attacked, beating on him with her little fists. "You snoop! You read my letters!"

Philip fended off the blows. "I wanted to know you and to find you. I was tremendously touched by them, loved your mother immediately, and was sorry for your situation."

She subsided, her face sad. "They are all I have left of her. When she died, Father discarded all her things."

"Jesus," he cried. "If the man was not already dead, I would crush him for not seeing what a treasure he had in you."

Fiona stared into the fire. "I keep waiting for him to reappear and berate me for my failures."

He put his arm around her. "Stop, Fiona. He will never be back. What he did before he went is best forgotten. The money can be worked out, and Cameron has no legitimate claim on you. You are free of both of them."

She glanced up, and he kissed her soft lips. The dear girl leaned against him, glad for loving, for comfort, and Philip felt the same. They kissed and cuddled, and it was soul satisfying.

"Philip," she whispered. "What if I had not met you? I have no one like you for a friend."

"And if I had not met you, I would be lonesome."

She touched his coat buttons. "Tell me who you really are."

"I am what you see, ma'am, just another sailor, come ashore."

"Yes," she sighed, "and I am Queen of the May."

"My word," he exclaimed, "I never realized."

They laughed, and Philip adored her.

****

Mr. Frisk presented himself, a sample card in hand. Fiona read it.

Suddenly, at home.

The Right Honble. The Viscount Greathouse, Roland Collingwood Seymour, 1759-1815

Burial from Two Twenty Green Street at Park Street to Heavenly Repose Cemetery, London

2 PM, May 10, 1815

Kindly bring this card.

She handed it back. "This is just right, Mr. Frisk."

"Well," he worried, "perhaps a bit terse, Miss Seymour?"

"Not at all, sir. My father had his preferences. How many of these will be sent?"

"Four."

She hid her fresh surprise. "To whom will they go?"

"Business associates Mr. Quiggs provided."

"Oh." Fiona digested this. "Thank you. Send them along. Everything else is all right?"

"Yes, ma'am, and the stone is on order. I, ah, assume you will only state name and dates? I suppose?"

"Indeed, Mr. Frisk. You think of every detail. Your services are most professional."

Frisk wriggled with pleasure. "Thank you so much. All is in readiness. I will take my leave but will be on hand tomorrow, to see all goes as it should."

"Thank you again. Good day."

He bowed himself out.

Fiona was upset, ashamed Philip should have heard. "Do you think us savages, Philip?" she groaned. "Such goings on! What a man, to have not a single friend. That is who he was, and I am a part of it all. An insane suitor, unknown debts, a death no one will mourn. This dismal house! It is an awful play, or a hideous novel. A charade of ruin!"

"All families are a mixed bag of bent nails," he drawled.

Fiona laughed gaily, lightening her distress. "You are too witty, Philip."

He stroked a finger down her cheek. "Am I, sweetheart?"

"Yes. I sink into a pit of despair, and you just swan along, untroubled. Tell me one true fact about yourself."

"It would necessarily be true, if it is a fact," he replied.

"How wise. Where did you go to school?" she inquired.

"Oxford."

"I see. I am a graduate of Miss Peabody's School for Young Ladies. I have been polished to a high degree of general ignorance. One more fact, please. Where is your home?"

"I have a little place near Southampton. What did you learn at Miss Peabody's?"

"Absolutely the least possible. For instance, newspapers are rife with items a lady should not know of. Novels may disturb the mind irreparably. Do not speak your opinions aloud or without consideration. Men may be listening and condemn you for wayward thinking. Never, ever complain. A husband appreciates, more than any charm, a docile, silent wife."

He shook his head.

"There were many lessons along that line," she said on. "Most succumbed. A few of us realized we were slowly being suffocated. I have seen Southampton on a map. It is rather far away from London."

"Not so far, if you sail."

How marvelous! "You keep a boat?"

Philip looked glum. "Well, I did."

Fiona gazed at him. "One moment. You said you were shipwrecked? Do you mean to say it was *your* ship? Not the navy's?"

"Clever girl."

"Ohhhh. You did some sort of secret thing; you were—Tell me you are not a spy."

"I am not a spy," he repeated.

"Well, what are you?"

"A man who is very fond of you. This emotion has multiplied in a very short time. But I trust the sentiment and hope you can trust me."

Fiona was perplexed. "I have not a crumb to steal, you know."

"I am not after crumbs. Yes, I have secrets I cannot tell you as yet. But I will, and I swear my conduct has been honorable. I still owe the navy my loyalty and my silence. Those obligations will ease in the next several days. In short, I am still on duty."

Her mind raced. "You were wrecked and landed in the water, you said, icy water. Then you became ill?"

"I was injured. Rigging fell on me, cracking my ribs. I had trouble breathing. This impeded lung action, and I developed pneumonia. See, I am a hero of the realm. Kiss me again."

Fiona happily did so. A hero! How fantastic. And there was a lot more to his story. She could not wait to hear it.

Philip congratulated himself for revealing only a strand of his yarn. Just as he was about to progress with Fiona, someone else appeared at the door.

"Oh, Quiggs, do come in," Fiona asked the gaunt, pallid fellow, an accountant if he ever saw one.

He ambled in sideways. "Miss Fiona, my deepest, etcetera," he muttered. "I am at your service."

"Do sit down. This is my friend, Mr. Laughton."

"Sir." The thin man folded himself into a chair.

"What I need to know, Quiggs, is if I am broke. Cameron was here yesterday and implied he holds all of my father's notes, his debts, or whatever. What can you tell me of my finances?"

The secretary cleared his throat. "Lord Cameron is a serpent in the grass, if I may say so, Miss Fiona. He slithers around and talks a jolly game of riches, but the man is a fraud coming and going. I warned the viscount of this flaw but could not make him listen. To that end, he invested in high-risk bonds on Lord Cameron's advice, and the market quickly sank to an ebb."

Quiggs sucked his cheeks ruefully. "To shorten the tale, Cameron is a thief and a cheat. He contrived ruin for your father, to gain his own ends. Ten thousand pounds are to be withdrawn from your father's accounts at the Bank of England on the morrow and transferred to him."

Fiona gasped. "Does he hold other obligations?"

"Not to my knowledge."

Philip spoke. "Fiona, did you obtain a death certificate?"

"Yes. Dr. Calvert signed it."

"Please go and get it."

Fiona hurried from the room.

"Quiggs," he instructed, "you will take the certificate immediately to the bank and speak to a bank officer. Show the certificate, say you are acting for the heirs, and have his accounts frozen until the will is read."

"Can I do this, sir?"

"Indeed you can. I was involved in a similar action recently on the death of my uncle."

Fiona returned with a paper and handed it to Quiggs, who perused it carefully.

"Go now, Quiggs." Philip searched his pocket and gave the man coins. "Catch a hackney, and come directly back to assure Miss Fiona all is well."

"Yes, sir. Right away." Quiggs lunged for the doors and was gone.

Fiona sat down, some breathless.

"You should have a capable solicitor, Fiona. Someone to straighten all this out. I recommend mine."

She just blinked.

Philip was angry, a state he avoided. "Cameron was bluffing. Bullying and threatening to keep you confused until this bond deal went through. The conniving bastard! I will see him sink to the bottom of his corruption."

"What of the marriage contract?" she asked. "Was he bluffing there, too?"

"I think not. He wants you for himself. I saw it in his face. He wheedled your father's money and by putting his back against a wall reckoned he could get you, too. It will not happen while I live." Damn if

Cameron would succeed; he would protect her, and he took her in his arms again. "Cameron will never touch you, Fiona. You deserve far better than him." Another sweet kiss. He nuzzled her ear and whispered, "Like me, for instance."

Fiona reveled in this closeness. Philip's kisses and sweet words were an escalating pleasure. Wait. Did he say…? Ha. She must be as saucy as he.

"And what would I do with a sailor and his secrets?" she teased.

"Enjoy yourself. Explore intimacies."

Her thoughts collided at the term, but she inquired, "What sort?"

He caressed her cheek, his hand large and warm. "All the things a man and a woman indulge in when alone."

She had a sudden surge of alarm, and her ears got hot.

He gazed intently into her face. "Fiona, you should understand that I am not taking your friendship, your trust, lightly. I feel a connection to you and have from the first. I am somewhat pressed, however. There are other things I should be doing than sitting on your sofa."

"Well," she huffed, "go do them. I know that I am a big box of trouble."

He shook his head. "My obligations cannot hold my attention. I wish to be with you."

"Or," she fretted on, "perhaps other ladies are waiting to see you home safe and dry."

He frowned. "Only you know about that wreck. I would ask that you do not mention it to anyone else."

Amazed, she asked, "Now I will be keeper of your

secrets?"

"Please, very briefly. I have already told you more than I should. And I have no interest in other ladies, you feisty girl."

She absolutely did not know what to think.

"Believe me, I would love to tell you everything," he insisted. "You mean a great deal to me, Fiona. Do not throw me out."

She quickly said, "I would never do that."

"You like me a little?" he asked, bringing her still closer.

"A little," she admitted. "I am frankly afraid to like you more."

"I will attend to that, my angel. Would you make love with me, Fiona?"

Fiona was struck dumb.

"Think about it," he whispered, his dark eyes boring holes into her. "Think of us together. All alone, exploring each other, saying what we feel."

He kissed her cheek and ear. "There has been no loving in your life, Fiona? Have you never—"

She leaned away from him. "Stop."

Instantly, he withdrew, like shutting a door. Then he smiled, and she hated him.

Wanting to put him in his place, she drew herself up, and smoothed her hair. "Very well. You may know I have not—that there has been no *loving*, as you choose to call it. I did not want to dance with the men I knew, so why in the world would I do anything else?" She gave him a small push. "And you recklessly sashay in with dozens of kisses, and I become shady."

He laughed.

"Trying to turn my head!" she cried. "You think I

am foolish? Next, no doubt, you will want more."

"Well, yes, I believe I said so," he confirmed. "But I did not say when."

"What?"

"You heard me."

Fiona, out of words, slumped back on the cushions.

"I adore you," Philip said, in a honeyed voice. "Is it not time for tea?"

****

Philip stuffed in cucumber sandwiches, jellied pear slices, iced shortbread, and a selection of nuts. He washed this down with a good blend of tea, Fiona serving him. Her green eyes glowed, he decided, as did her skin. She was almost a redhead but not quite. Her dusting of freckles was endearing. She resembled the portrait he had seen, of the woman in court dress.

"Who is depicted in the large portrait in the foyer, Fiona?"

"My maternal grandmother, Madelaine Elliot Pembroke Greville. She was a cousin of George III, and this irked Father no end, only a lowly viscount. I think it spurred him to crave a higher rank. A shame *he* could not marry a fortune and a more exalted title."

"If the lady was a royal cousin, then so are you, Fiona."

"Oh, sorry, but there are packs of us, all distant, and of little importance." She waved a hand. "Sown like wildflowers."

"What happens to your father's title?"

"There is no male heir. The title will go into abeyance, which made him furious."

Philip wanted to ask her opinion of titles, but it would seem he had just heard it. She did not particularly care and liked *him*, an ordinary seaman in her view. He wanted to hug himself. What could be better than close relations without the tiresome trappings of rank?

"If you appeared at court in all your beauty, Fiona, you would add a dash of glory to their humdrum lives."

"Mercy! Do not talk so," she joked, "or off to the Tower with you."

"You may keep that secret as well."

"I will, sir."

Her smiling good cheer was a rare blessing. *God help me*, Philip mused, *are you daft, man? Stop falling in thrall with this winsome creature, this beguiling girl. You are too old and worn out. You cannot, should not.* To fend off this indecision, he kissed her again. She melted in his arms. He was caught in a very choppy sea, and his helm could not hold steady.

****

Quiggs returned and produced both the death certificate and a form showing the Greathouse accounts frozen as of this date, duly stamped and signed.

The man was visibly gratified. "It went just as you said, sir. The certificate was sufficient to have them hold any transactions on the accounts until they are notified the will has been read."

Fiona was most pleased. "Thank you, Quiggs."

"Good work," Philip echoed.

"But is there a will?" she asked.

Quiggs nodded. "Yes, miss, there is. In your father's library safe."

She gasped. "There is a safe?"

He unfolded himself and stood. "I will show you."

Fiona hung back. "Well, I—thank you, Quiggs, but

I do not care to go into the library until tomorrow. I will see about it then. At two of the clock or so, we will leave for the cemetery. I do not expect anyone will come."

"I shall be honored to attend, Miss Fiona. I worked for the viscount fifteen years and will say farewell as I should."

"I hope you will stay on, Quiggs. Until I sink into poverty."

"Oh," he ventured, glancing at Philip, "I very much doubt that outcome. I will go now and return on the morrow."

"Tell me, Quiggs," Phillip asked. "Fiona says the title will lapse, but is anything entailed?"

"No, sir, nothing."

"Thank you again," Fiona said. "You have been a great help. Goodbye."

Fiona marveled as the secretary went. "I never knew Quiggs was so nice. A *safe*, Philip. What about that? I imagine it will be crammed with worthless bonds."

"Or his rock collection."

"Violets pinned to old invitation cards. Colored ribbons. Chocolates. He liked chocolates but thought they made him fat. Something did. His tailor worked hard to escape his temper. *Cannot be accurate*, Father would shout. *Measure again*." It made her rather sad to remember. "And a will is in there, according to Quiggs. Leaving me nothing, I suppose. I may get to keep all my lavish gowns and slippers. Knowing Father, it will be some sort of rude surprise."

"Not to worry," Philip suggested. "It has been written in some fashion. You cannot change what is already done."

"Yes, worry about what might happen, not what is." She breathed a laugh. "You shall make a philosopher of me, Phillip. Miss Peabody would strenuously object."

"Good. I aim to free you from her clutches."

"At last! Revolution."

He stroked his finger along her cheek. "Then, being your elder, I can teach you what you need to know."

It gave her a shaky tremor. "How old are you, Grandfather?"

"Six and twenty." His dark eyes gazed into hers. "But I have covered a lot of ocean since I was your age."

She sorted out this remark. "You mean you have seen the world and I have not? I read good books and have improved my store of knowledge. I imagine myself in other lives and situations and act as I should. I have my adventures and a good mind. I can think."

He just looked doubtful.

It riled her. "And I fully intended to run away and create a new life in Surrey. All on my own, because it is not far and would be inexpensive. To find I had no money put an end to that, but I was ready to go, to take my chances. Then you came along and here we are. But, believe me—"

"I do believe you. You are the bravest woman I have ever known."

"Oh." She sniffed. "Big fib."

"You are beautiful inside and out, Fiona, made of taffeta, crushed velvet, and rose petals. I must go."

Fiona was taken aback. "What? You say these

tremendous things, then *leave?*"

"I must attend a meeting. Another navy thing. Three in all, then I will cut myself loose and tell you everything."

This man! "Am I to accept…um, I must ask, is this some kind of emotional flimflam?"

"You delicious creature," he murmured and began again with the kisses.

It stole her breath and erased her doubts. He was wonderful, wonderful, ran through her mind like music. "You will come tomorrow? I know funerals are dismal. You do not have to."

"I will be here, love. Wait for me."

"Oh, dear. I will dine alone tonight, then teach myself more chess."

"Ah, do you play chess?"

"I am learning. You are either a king or a bishop, Philip. Probably a bishop, because they move diagonally."

They stood and strolled to the doors.

"I am no chess piece, Fiona. What are you, to cast such an amorous spell over me in such a short time? An enchantress?"

"I should be so lucky. No, I am only me. The friend of a seaman, who keeps sailing away."

"I will be back on an early tide. As I said, wait for me."

Oh, his handsome face, his amber eyes, that mouth. "Yes. I will."

He opened the doors to Sumpter, busily dusting the tall clock.

"I will be back tomorrow around noon, Fiona. Take the day easy. All these troubles will fade away."

"I will think of that, Philip. Until then."

He bent to kiss her hand, and a little thrill went up her arm. He took his hat, smiled, and Sumpter showed him out. Philip's leaving seemed to take the air out of the room.

A large pit opened up in Fiona's consciousness. Philip was gone.

****

Philip strolled up Green Street to Park Lane, his mind on Fiona Seymour. She had taken up residence in his head and stayed with him when they parted. That had never happened before, with any woman. Fiona was a flower, opening fresh and untouched, or a wood sprite, rusty-haired and mischievous. Female, wholly female. Elemental, making other women seem a hollow façade. The idea of her father selling her off twisted his gut. Some vulgar sod putting his hands on her was unthinkable. He wanted to shelter her, keep her safe, and really know her.

He caught a hackney and rode to St. James Street and White's. Alighted, strolled in, and as ever, Burgess manned the front desk. A fair-haired, wiry fellow, his face widened into a smile.

"Why, I declare, Lord Colbourne. It has been many a day, sir."

"How goes it, Burgess? You are looking well."

"I thank you, my lord. I go on, though aged."

Philip handed over his hat. "I cannot see it. I am here to have a drop."

"Very good, sir."

He sauntered down the hall and past the dining room, empty at this early hour. The card room contained a few members, none of whom he knew. In the lounge he took a seat facing the door and ordered a large whiskey. Sipped it, thinking of Fiona's green eyes, and those flecks of gold. The way her straight brows expressed her mood. Her temper, her fierce independence. How she had managed with her ogre of a papa, he did not know. Women survived on very little. Fiona had strength. Cousin of a king, he mused. Breeding will tell, eh?

In the midst of these ramblings, a familiar face appeared. The man took in his presence, flashed a smile, and hastened over. Philip stood and offered his hand. "Bradford, good to see you."

"Colbourne, old man, what a thing. Where have you been for months and years?"

"Take a chair. Down in Hampshire. Had a spot of pneumonia and whatnot. Laid me low. In town to see my medical man."

Bradford studied him. "You look well. Tanned and that."

"Nothing to do for weeks but sun myself." Bradford was always too shrewd by half. "But what of you?"

"Stocks and bonds. Bonds and stocks, all the day long. M'father kicked off and left me the whole shebang." The waiter brought the man a brandy, and he sipped.

Philip decided to play a card. "I am doing damn all. Life seems to be in suspension. The endless war drags on and on."

A curtain descended; Philip felt it.

"I did my time," Bradford asserted. "Shrapnel in the thigh, and that was that. Hurts when it rains, and it always rains. I say fight on until Nappy is dead with his head on a pike. I do not give a shit how long it takes to get him."

"Well said, Bradford. I thank you for your sacrifice. I just get down about it."

"I made it back. Many did not." The man downed his glass. "Well, Colbourne, hope your health returns. See you."

He stood up and briskly walked away. Bradford had turned cold at the mention of the war lingering too long. Philip must be cautious, mind what he said, and not hurry a conversation. Well, practice helped in this spy game, for which he was damn unsuited. Bradford would now think him dogmeat.

Philip drank his whiskey, gave up on White's as a hotbed of information, and left the club. A visit later in the evening might prove more useful. He hailed another hackney and rode home considering what a coil Malrose had gotten him into. Otherwise, he could be at Two Twenty Green Street, kissing Fiona and admiring her lush little breasts. Which he must soon fondle or die of longing. Jesus. In two days, she had taken over his brain.

****

Fiona wandered about, in and out of the house and garden. As twilight fell, she moseyed through the lower rooms. If this house became hers, she would throw out the furniture and rugs, the horrid drapes, and all of it. Paint and paper and choose articles which would please both her eye and her preferences.

As she poked at a solitary dinner, the room closed in on her. The evening stretched out endlessly. She could not go out for a walk in the dark. *Have you no occupation*, Father had scolded. No, she did not. It made her morose.

She climbed the stairs to her room, sat at her dressing table, and gazed into the foggy glass. The engagement ball invitation propped against it beckoned. Her pretty new gown, where would she ever wear it now? Anna Featherstone had been a friend. Fiona hungered for company and a crowd to lose herself in. The house creaked with her father's spirit, trapping her inside its walls.

Why could she not go to the ball? No one knew her father was lying in the library, cold as a fish. Who cared, anyway? She yearned to get out, see people, assure herself *she* was alive and had a place in the world. Otherwise, she might disappear like smoke, and no one would even notice. She rang for Daisy and sorted through a drawer of chemises.

Fiona fetched her peach gown from the dressing room, a triumph of workmanship by her modiste. She wrestled herself from her outer clothing, tugged up her stays, smoothed her chemise, and stepped into the silk folds.

Daisy tapped at the door and entered. "Something, miss?"

"Yes, please. Help with this gown. I am going out to the Featherstones' ball. Just for an hour or so. And you must come with me as a chaperone, being my auntie, since I have no escort."

A look of consternation from the maid.

"I have to get out of this house!" Fiona cried. "It will be just like when we went to the Music Fair. You were a great success."

Daisy wrung her hands. "But miss, that was in the daytime!"

"What difference does that make?"

"It was crowded, I wore your hat, and no one spoke to me."

"This ball will also be crowded, and no attention will be paid."

"Can you promise—"

"Not to worry! I need my hair done. Please, Daisy. I will see you are not embarrassed."

A hangdog expression crossed Daisy's features. "Just this once, miss."

Fiona again sat at the dressing table, and the maid pulled out pins. Her hair fell heavily to her shoulders and back. Daisy brushed and braided, arranged a cluster of loops and twists, and soon Fiona looked very well. She pinched her cheeks and rose to slip her feet into matching peach slippers.

"Such a gown, miss. Quite shows you off."

Fiona eyed the neckline, which was cut very low. Once again, she hitched up the stays, plumping her breasts. *Let them all look*, she thought with determination, *but they will never touch. I am off the market.* "Thank you, Daisy. You are a jewel. Go and put on that Sunday silk gown you favor. Then come back."

"Oh, miss…"

"Quickly!"

Daisy slumped away.

Fiona dashed back down the stairs to find the butler, who was sorting the late post.

"Sumpter, would you call for the carriage? I am going out."

The man raised thin, questioning brows.

"Just for an hour or so, with Daisy. Tell Jem, if you

will."

"Yes, miss."

"Is there anything for me?"

"Indeed, miss." He handed over cards. "The rest are for the viscount."

"Well, give them to Quiggs when he comes tomorrow. Thank you." Fiona felt compelled to explain. "If I do not leave this house for a time, I will go mad."

He bowed slightly in understanding. "Yes, Miss Fiona. I will inform Jem."

Back up the stairs, Daisy appeared, and Fiona straightened the maid's plain black silk gown, which seemed most suitable for an auntie. The maid's curling hair did not need much. Fiona added a necklace of mixed stones, and her fine paisley shawl, and even Daisy was pleased by the effect.

Fiona tucked the invitation into her reticule along with a hanky, and the shillings clinked. With her flowered silk shawl over her shoulder, she and her curiously arrayed companion set out down the hall to the stairs. Sumpter waited below and gave Daisy a curious look, but the maid only smiled vacantly.

"The carriage is here, miss."

"Thank you, Sumpter."

She and Daisy breezed out the front door into the welcome darkness, and Fiona felt a free person. Only a speck in the great city, but she could survive. London was her home, and she was a competent woman, on her own. That felt very fine. She called to the coachman, "Hays Mews at Water Street, please, Jem."

"Aye, Miss Fiona."

The footman, Walsh, helped them in, sprang to the box with Jem, and off they went. Fiona was highly excited to be so unconstrained. Father would not hound her, Cameron would be righteously squashed like overripe fruit, and she would live her life as she wished. Daisy watched the world go by the carriage window but said nothing.

They soon reached their destination, the large house brightly lit in every window, carriages in a line. Jem took a place, and they slowly crept forward, routine at a large gathering. Fiona saw couples and groups, dressed to the nines, parade up the walk and into the open front doors. Their turn came, and a liveried footman assisted her and her "auntie" to the pavement.

"We should not be long, Jem."

"Aye, miss, we will abide."

"Look confident, Daisy dear, and no one will stop us."

"Yes, miss," the maid whispered.

Fiona raised her chin defiantly, and they strolled to the doors. There was a crush at the receiving line, and she saw Anna among them. Fiona waited until she had a chance to speak to her friend, but that did not come.

The two women were jostled aside by a horde of well-wishers and, having no escort, were paid no attention at all. No servant asked to announce them. She stepped away, Daisy followed, and somewhat perturbed, Fiona turned down the hallway and toward the ballroom.

That enormous space was even more jammed with merrymakers. Dancers swirled in rainbow colors, the chandeliers sparkled, music blared. Liquor, food, and myriad other perfumes hung invisibly in the air. Feet shuffled and stamped the polished floor, conversation hummed. Daisy clutched her elbow, her expression alarmed.

Both of them put off by the clamor, Fiona skirted behind a row of potted shrubs and found chairs behind them. Daisy fell into one. Fiona sat to catch a breath and peeped out from behind the spikey foliage.

Startled, she quickly drew back. Not ten feet away, the evil Cameron stood talking with that notorious roué, Lord Harley. Thankfully, they parted, going opposite directions. She must be vigilant and dare not wander around. He would see her, raise a ruckus, and tell everyone she was grossly disrespectful to the dead.

Fiona's heart bumped. Oh, mercy, she should never have come!

****

Philip stepped down from his carriage, and Gerson, his coachman, pulled forward to await his return. He strolled up the walk, took one look at the clogged foyer, eased around the crowd, and proceeded down a hallway toward the music. He glanced in the ballroom doors to see people packed in like herrings and kept walking. At a short distance, he located the card room. A dozen or so men lounged at tables, enjoying various games of chance.

In a corner, he saw Lord Meacham, his foppish appearance about the same as years before. Garbed in evening black, he sported a loud brocade vest and a ruffled lace cravat. Elaborate, pinched curls of various shades adorned his head. His disgusted expression confirmed he was losing. He threw down his cards, rose from the table, and unsteadily headed for the door. Philip nonchalantly followed.

"Whiskey," Meacham called to a waiter. The man

hurried to serve him. He drank it down and squeezed his lips together.

Philip paid no mind to him and said, "A large whiskey, if you please."

"Yes, sir."

Meacham cut a glance his way as the man fetched it.

"Evening," Philip said. "How are you?"

"Hunh." He pushed his tumbler to the waiter. "Another."

"I say," Philip said, taking his glass and ignoring Meacham's bad temper, "I believe we have met."

"Eh?"

"Some time ago. I am Philip Laughton, Earl of Colbourne."

He blearily acknowledged this. "Uh. Lord Meacham, your servant, sir. Good to see you."

"The same. I do not get to London often of late. Nice to see a familiar face."

"Yah, thas so. Town full of bloody soldiers." His expression sagged, and he became maudlin. "War snatched 'em away, all the old fellows. Colton, right. Would have known you in a sec."

Philip moved closer to the man. Meacham was pissed drunk.

"Who else is around from the old days?" he asked.

Meacham leaned heavily to one side. "Nobody. The war, the war. Ending soon, mark my word. Ending, yes, by God."

"I sincerely hope so, sir. I have no use for the war going on and on forever. Needs to stop. Any way it can be done."

Meacham focused a wandering eye and poked him

with a finger. "Got a pal you should meet, Bolton. Jus' the man."

"Who would that be?" Philip asked.

The baron began to sway. Philip handed off his glass.

"Who?" he repeated.

Meacham's face turned a sickly green. "Go...get, get...Cameron. Gonna be...sick."

To his disgust, Meacham bent over, vomited, wobbled sideways, and fell down in the mess. Philip quickly stepped away as a cry was raised and made it out the door to the hall, thoroughly shocked. Cameron! *Cameron*, for Christ's sake. He could knock them all off at once. Three birds with one stone.

He lingered in an alcove, behind a giant urn full of peacock feathers. Presently, here came not only Cameron, but he recognized Lord Harley, rushing down the hallway. The two halted and exchanged anxious words.

"Did he say anything?" Cameron hissed.

"I cannot know," Harley whispered.

"Take the fool out of here promptly. We will meet later."

Harley turned into the card room, and Cameron kept walking. Philip pondered what to do. Report to Malrose. Yes, take no action, just state what you have seen and heard. He attracted no notice as two footmen supported Meacham from the card room, Harley attending.

Philip darted through a door and found himself at the side of the teeming ballroom. He took account of his location, stepped along the wall, circled a forest of potted shrubs, and went on toward the main doors. The foyer was empty. He exited the house unnoticed and at the walkway, raised an arm. His carriage pulled out and came around to take him up. Philip called, "Home, Gerson," climbed in and the carriage trundled away.

He was safe. Meacham had not been able to get his name right and was too drunk to remember him. Philip considered the evening a resounding success. He had gained vital information, and not a soul he knew had seen him.

****

A tall man stepped through the side door to Fiona's left. In the light from a brace of sconces, she clearly saw him. Her mouth opened in startled surprise, followed by a rapid dismay that wrapped tightly around her throat.

There stood that cad, *Philip Laughton*, if that was indeed his name. He stood out from the other men nearby, his height, his air of assurance. Self-possessed and confident, he was polished in his grand yet informal stance, as if a prince. But he was not! He was one of *them*, the predators who sifted through the eager girls, then chose one to cheat on and make miserable. How nasty and cruel of him to play such games with her.

Who is he, what is he, Fiona pondered as he stealthily passed by her hiding place, never looking her way. She recalled every moment, the coins he easily handed out, his fine clothes, the stately house on Park Street. His bleeding *secrets*! God above, he was an imposter of some stripe, a liar and a scoundrel. Kissing her until she went all steamy, putting his big hands on her person. Saying those things. And he had the valise, and her precious letters.

Not for long, not for one day more. She had taken a

91

wrong step, had gone too far with the heartless, smooth talker. She would go to his house, get her property back, and kick him in the shins if he tried to stop her. Ha. If he was a sailor, she was Cleopatra.

"Daisy, we must leave here at once."

"Why? We have got ourselves here. I was hoping for a glass of—"

"No, we must leave immediately. I was wrong to come."

Daisy wrapped herself in the shawl and stood. Fiona wearily rose to her feet, and the women made their way through the throng to the front doors. No one observed her, no one spoke her name. She plodded down the walk, Daisy by her side, and Jem, on the watch, saw them and urged the horses forward. Walsh helped Daisy in, and Fiona murmured, "Tell Jem I would go home now, thank you."

"Yes'm."

The door closed, and in a moment, the carriage rumbled away over the cobbles. She did not feel sorrow or disappointment or shame. Just an emptiness. It had been a horrid few days, but she would go on, stronger than before, and depend upon herself in all things. Because now Fiona knew that was all she had.

****

Arriving home, Philip penned a note to Malrose.

Suspect third man Lord Cameron. Close contact, cryptic remarks with other two at Featherstone ball.

C.

He walked out to the hall. He would have a footman take the note to Malrose first thing. Restless, he left the house and walked to Green Street. If lights were visible, perhaps Fiona would still be up. He longed to be with her again.

The place was alight. He waited for an approaching carriage to pass before crossing the street, but the vehicle halted at the curb in front of Two Twenty. Philip stepped back into the shadows, in case it was Cameron. Then he heard Fiona's light voice. The carriage moved on, and he saw her, in a fairy shade of pastel ballgown. It was Fiona, dressed to kill!

What the hell was she doing out alone? No, another woman was with her. A dreadful thought struck him. Jesus, could the girl have something going on with that bastard Cameron? Has he somehow been played? *It cannot be.* These were traitors who would slit her throat without a qualm! Surely, there was an explanation.

His anger spiked. They had sunk his ship! She did not realize the turncoat's aims. Or she did.

No, this was crazed. She could not fake those kisses, those tender words. Was it mad to think—Only two days and he was in mud up to the knees!

Philip walked back home feeling old, tired, spent, and ill again. He coughed raggedly. Goddamn her, he would thrash the chit. No, he would not. But it felt good to think of spanking her bare bottom for whatever she had done. Because, by the devil, she had done something!

Chapter Five

Wednesday

After she woke, Fiona drank her cup of chocolate, then enjoyed a bath. Daisy washed her long hair, such a bother. After all was done, Fiona sat in her robe before the fire, brushing out her drying hair.

Daisy searched over her wardrobe. "There is naught black for you, miss. Not even a dark blue."

"I do not like dark colors and will wear what I have. I am sure no one is coming to the funeral anyway. And I am a dead thing in the starchy ton, so why bother?"

"Is it so, miss?"

Fiona recalled the pain of feeling invisible. "That ball last night was awful. A big crush of noisy people, loud music, and bad air. I have decided not to go back to the daily parade." She brushed faster. "The ton is all empty glitter, and I am *not* trying to find a husband. Father's hopes I would marry into wealth and power have fallen away. I will now do what I want."

Daisy just stared.

"So, bring my yellow muslin, and I shall shine like the sun."

The maid went to fetch it. *Oh*, Fiona thought guiltily, *I am wicked clear through to the back of me.*

All this time, she did not spare a thought for Philip

Laughton, the poser. The hanger-about at balls. She had never seen him there before, because he was at sea, or so he said. Ha. He might have been in jail. He could even be married. This idea stuck a knife in her heart.

When dressed, she hastened down to the foyer. Sumpter was accepting the delivery of a large wreath, woven of flowering branches, lobed leaves, and various stiff blooms.

"Mercy, Sumpter, who sent that?"

He read the attached card. "The firm of Gleason and Sons, Brokers."

"Oh, well, prop the thing against the library door." She smoothed her skirt. "If Mr. Laughton should chance to come by, please say I am not at home. Not to anyone but Quiggs."

Up went the thin brows.

Fiona did not wish to make an excuse. "Thank you, Sumpter."

"Yes, miss."

She went on to breakfast and ate a delicious meal, served by a cheerful Gregg. Daisy arrived with warm apple buns, so all was well in the kitchens. *By heaven,* Fiona considered, biting into one, *I can manage all this. When Quiggs comes, I will get more information.* The safe! She would have a look in there, never mind her father's remains.

All this must be treated as an adventure, she reckoned, sipping her coffee. Rapacious men like Cameron were of no consequence among the hedges she must jump. There would be challenges. Useless to worry over them, wait and see. Stay calm. Carry on with dignity.

Fiona choked back sudden tears. Stood, thanked

the servants, and went out to her garden, to search for consolation and for weeds.

****

Despite unsettled thoughts, Philip slept deeply through the night. As soon as he woke, however, his mind turned to roasting Fiona Seymour over hot embers until she told him exactly what she was up to. Her whole story might be a tissue of lies, from taking a nosedive in front of the bank, to passionate kisses on that tapestry sofa. Maybe she had known all along who he was and plotted ways to extort funds from him. Outrageous.

Really, he grumbled, washing and dressing himself, she might have pushed her father, or an inconvenient husband, down that flight of stairs. He had not seen the body and how would he know who had died? He had never met the viscount. Philip shrugged into his coat. The butler had seemed decent. Honest face and manner, all that. He went downstairs, furious.

In the dining room, Mrs. Reston waited, gushing good cheer. "Good morning, my lord. A truly fine day, not a cloud above."

I have one right here, he silently groused, but said, "Wondrous. When is Pearce coming?"

"He should arrive today, sir." She adjusted her frilled cap. "Most unexpected, you know, your arrival."

"No matter, Missus. I managed without a valet at sea."

"Oh, sir," she lamented, "such hardship you must have endured."

This remark was an understatement. Reston appeared, carrying a silver tray, and Philip's breakfast was placed before him. The fat sausages, kipper, and coddled eggs drew his interest, as did a plate of scones. Philip ate heartily, his mind working over the Fiona dilemma. He would tell her nothing. Certainly not mention he had seen her returning from a late-night gala. While in mourning! Tantamount to severe disregard for the common rules of funereal decorum. Unless she had kept a quiet lover's tryst. He stabbed a sausage with his fork. What the blazes did he care?

Philip drained his coffee cup, and Reston poured another. By God, he would take that damnable valise to her and have done with it. Soon, Cameron would be taken away in shackles, and maybe Fiona, too. He munched another scone. Blast it, he could see no good outcome to this. His portion of trust had gone dry, and he sensed imminent attack brewing on all sides. He would not be scuttled again! No, indeed, he would not.

Full of resolve, he tidied his person and put on his hat. Lifted the blasted valise and strode out the front door with a fixed purpose.

He marched along, sick of betrayal, treachery, and duplicity. He had gazed into the face of the courier who had handed him the oilskin packet and seen nothing amiss. Had taken the wheel and turned the ship, unaware of what was coming, no more than the doomed man he had left on the French shore.

Two Twenty Green Street appeared deserted, but Philip knew that Fiona was in the house. He could almost hear her breathing as he lifted and dropped the knocker.

Sumpter promptly opened the door. "Oh. Mr. Laughton," he murmured.

"In the flesh. Fetch Miss Fiona, I have something of hers."

The butler hesitated nervously.

Philip raised his voice. "If the girl has the temerity to pretend she is not at home," he continued, "be assured I am having none of it. Send her along, or I will throw this valise into the Thames."

Sumpter asserted his righteousness. "Miss Fiona is in mourning, Mr. Laughton. Her feelings are drawn taut."

"So are mine. I would not enjoy using force, Sumpter, but I will take—" A movement caught his eye. Here came the little vixen, scampering down the hall, a ray of sunshine in her yellow gown.

"I would have that valise, if you please, sir."

The sight of her irritated him further. "And I will say that it is all there, including the satin stays."

Sumpter glanced to the floor. Fiona's cheeks turned bright pink.

"Vicious slander and abject falsehood! No gentleman would mention such."

"And no lady would cruise about town with a case full of unmentionables. That I just mentioned."

Her voice trembled with resentment. "I saw you last night, you rogue and imposter! On your navy business, gussied up in borrowed clothes, at a *ball*! Not a word you have said to me has been true."

"And I might charge you with the same, little miss. I saw *you*, returning in the late hours, in your finery. Out on the town, eh? Larking about while your recently lamented reclines in the library! Or at least, so you indicated. I did not see him."

"I assure you, sir," the exasperated butler cut in, "that the viscount is dead as the apostles! I must ask you to leave, or I will call for a constable."

Fiona grabbed at the valise.

Philip held it away. "Not until you tell me the truth," he threatened. "Are you in league with Cameron and his cronies?"

Fiona suddenly wilted, her face baffled. "Are you insane?"

"I have reason to believe that he is involved in nefarious dealings."

"How astute of you! I have told you what he is. He cheated my father and would have me locked in lifelong servitude. Cameron is despicable in the extreme."

"There is more to it than that."

"I do not know what you are speaking of. Give me the valise. Please."

Philip dropped it with a clunk.

Sumpter closed the door. "Shall I call for tea, Miss Fiona?"

She frowned. "Why not? The man has never eaten."

"I have breakfasted and do not want tea," Philip stated. "Let us sit down and you can tell me something true."

"That I am prepared to hate and despise you?" she scoffed.

He took the obstinate girl's elbow, guided her into the drawing room and shut the doors behind him.

She jerked away. "How dare you handle me!"

"Have a seat." How could he be angry with her? She was fabulous all in yellow, her hair quite red in contrast. She smelled of flowery soap. Every fiber of his being wanted to reach out and hold her in his arms. "We need to talk."

She flounced away and sat on the sofa by the fire. "Five minutes. I have important things to do."

"First of all," Philip began, sitting beside her, "did you know me when we met? Who I was?"

"How could I know anything about a ramshackle sailor?" she protested. "You coaxed me into that hackney. I know what your aim was. You thought me *available*, took me to that house, and ordered me to take off articles of my clothing."

"So I was a stranger?" he persisted.

"You still are!"

He gazed into her quite green eyes. She was angry and hurt. His suspicions fell away and he sat back. "I assumed that was what you were out on the street for, Fiona. Then I thought you were in on the plot."

"What plot, you lunatic?"

Dammit anyway, he had gone this far. He had to straighten things between them. "I had better start at the beginning."

"Four minutes left," she huffed.

Philip looked down at his open hands and began to speak. "I have, for some time, been engaged in a dangerous game, having to do with the war."

Fiona became alert.

"I am a captain in the Royal Navy, but my position is unusual. I entered an arrangement whereby I would sail my own ship, the *Calliope*, a trim, forty-foot sloop, back and forth across the channel. Generally at night, Dover to Calais. I flew no flag and was taken for a fisherman, all hung about with nets and so on. We were lucky, and I had a fine crew."

He glanced at Fiona, who was listening raptly.

"I carried papers, various documents, and often,

people. The last months were busy. We made extra trips to deliver whatever we were charged with and accept what we were given. On the last of these jaunts, I was passed an oilskin of papers. Headed back to Dover, the sun just rising, we were overtaken by a fast French cutter and fired upon. We were lightly armed, preferring speed."

Philip relived it all, the noise, the haste, yelling orders. "The crew rushed to uncover, prime, and fire the two light cannon we carried. Under all possible sail, we made a run for it. My men manned the cannon, and at the wheel, I sharply maneuvered our course. Our cannon fired, but it was too late. The cutter sailed closer, let loose a barrage, and we were hit amidships, blowing my three sailors to hell. Dismasted, the spars and rigging fell on me, and I lost consciousness."

He had to pause, remembering the tragedy, the smashing blow, falling, the ship on fire.

"When I came to, I crawled out from under debris. There was no sign of my men or the cutter. We had been left to burn and sink. The ship was listing badly, heavily down in the stern and partly under water, but that had doused the fire. Unable to stand and absorb the rocking of the craft, I hauled myself up, caught a rope, and tied myself to the wheel."

Philip wiped away the moisture in his eyes. "The wind came up, and the water turned rough. I used my weight to hold the craft steady and in the right direction. I reckoned I was some few miles off the English coast and hoped I could manage to hang on. The ship continued to slowly sink, and soon I was scudding along on a tide, half under water. I feared I would pass out again, but I was so close!

"I had to hold steady with everything I had and ride it out. I prepared to face death as the sea churned, was taken by a strong inbound current, and then, the sloop went down with a whoosh"—he snapped his fingers—"just like that. I caught a line wrapped around a spar, kept my head up, clung to it, and—" He paused again.

"Oh, Philip," Fiona whispered.

"Time passed as I struggled to stay afloat. Then I could see the white cliffs shining. The tide lifted me and my spar like flotsam and tossed us forward and forward. I had almost made it to Dover harbor, ships were in sight. In a final, great surge, I washed up about a quarter mile out near fellows unloading cargo from a barge. Somehow, I do not quite remember, they rescued me.

"But my troubles were not over. I suffered from exposure, cracked ribs, cuts and bruises. The papers I carried from France were handed off to the right man, although I was somewhat out of my head. In hospital, with my chest bound up, I could not breathe properly and developed a pneumonia. Sick and feverish, I prepared to die yet again."

It all washed over him like the cold sea. "I had lost everything, Fiona," he grieved. "My crew, my fine ship, and now my health. But tough as leather, I slowly recovered, as you see. But deeply depressed and exhausted, I felt I was coming home to nothing and could not see the way ahead. I came to London to attend to family business at the bank. Then I met you."

"Oh," she breathed.

"But who were you? A pretty trickster, who fell down for a living? Tempting some foolish man like me to stand you to a meal? What else would you do for a few pounds? I took you home to see. To maybe find some respite, if you were in my bed."

Fiona believed him entirely. His words, the pained look on his face, his evident sorrow. Pity for him rose up. "I am so sorry, Philip, for your losses. How terrible it must have been. How brave you were."

"Well, more like desperate. If I let go of the wheel, the ship would keel over and go down for certain. My men were gone. Jesus, there was not a rag left to bring home to their families." He sadly grimaced. "I have since learned we were betrayed. The courier that handed me the papers was killed, and the cutter took out after us, to make sure the packet strapped to my chest would never reach England."

Fiona was ashamed to have doubted him. Philip was a champion! "Thank God it is over."

She saw him weigh his words.

"Well, that is the thing. It is not over. I have been charged with another duty by my superior. I went to that ball last night to seek out the ones who saw to it my ship and crew were lost. I have also learned the French were tipped off by Englishmen with investments in France. Traitors, Fiona, who want the war over, and will do anything to see it done."

"You know them?"

"Slightly."

Fiona drew a breath. "Who are they?"

"I cannot tell you that."

She tried another tack. "Do I know them?"

"Quite likely."

"Mercy! They are members of the ton?"

"Quit prying, girl."

Again, they closely regarded each other.

"Allow me to help," she offered. "I stand ready to do whatever I might to aid you."

He smiled indulgently.

"I mean it, Philip. I know everyone in the ton. At least many of them, the ones who hang about at balls and such."

"These men are deadly."

"They certainly are! Believe me, I have learned to avoid the worst of them like the plague. You cannot imagine what skills women cultivate to keep themselves to themselves."

"I warned you about the ton."

"Thank you so much, but you did not mention grabby hands. Give me a task."

"Kiss me."

Then it struck her. "Wait! Was my father a part of this?"

A shadow crossed his face. "His name was not mentioned."

"God in heaven! Did you know who *I* was when we met? Has this all been a snare, and if he had not died—"

"Fiona, my dear."

It was very troubling. Traitors! "Well, I do not know what he did, with money, with his time. He never confided in me."

"Not to worry. I have reported what I learned last night. Maybe it will be enough facts to proceed, then they do not need me. What are the chances of lunch?"

Fiona softly laughed. "Very good."

They shared a fine lunch. Philip had found comfort in telling Fiona of his saga. It lightened the load somehow. A few tidbits about his mission could surely do no harm. Blast it, he was not a spy, but a go-between. He would return home soon and see if a missive had arrived from Malrose. He had already had enough of this cloak-and-dagger affair. He had promptly provided the third name, so what else did Malrose require of him?

Back in the drawing room, Philip polished choice love words to a shine. He would whisper them in Fiona's charming ear, and...

A tap at the doors. Fiona called, "Come."

Sumpter showed in Mr. Quiggs. "Miss Fiona, Mr. Laughton. Good day."

"Good day, Mr. Quiggs," Fiona greeted the man. "Do have a seat."

"Thank you. I wanted to be in good time. It is just now one of the clock."

"No one has come. I do not expect any callers. A wreath came earlier from one of his brokerage houses."

"In early times," Philip commented, "folks would hire professional mourners to raise a crowd."

"How funny." She laughed. "To sing the praises of the dead?"

"Exactly."

"Not at all the thing," Quiggs soberly remarked.

"When I die," Fiona declared, "I hope I have lived a good life and therefore will have many friends to weep and howl at my passing. Just a little."

Philip smiled at her innocence.

"The hour advances," Quiggs reminded them. "Sumpter gave me the morning post, and I was hoping to enter the library. I could open the safe and give you that key."

"Yes, the will." She nibbled her lower lip. "Then

let us go."

"May I come too?" he asked.

"Oh, please, Philip."

They all trooped out the doors and down the hall. Quiggs moved aside the garish wreath and opened the heavy library door. The room was chill, the windows thrown open. There was the odor of mold and wet greenery. The closed coffin stood on a long table, flowers banked around it. Fiona stood uncertainly in the middle of the room. Quiggs placed letters on the wide desk and stepped to the long bookcase. Philip leaned on the wall, interested.

"It is just here, Miss Fiona, behind this plaque." Quiggs swung a brass plaque engraved with a wreath aside to reveal a box safe built into the wall. The man produced a key, turned it in the lock, pulled the handle down, and the safe door swung open.

Quiggs made a choked sound. Fiona walked forward, and Philip stepped to see. Rows of gold coins lay in trays, flanked by bound stacks of notes, a bundle of what appeared to be bonds, and more bills, loose in the bottom. It was highly unexpected.

"Quiggs," Fiona cried, "what is all this?"

"The coins were there all along," he answered, his manner stunned, "but this other—the viscount must have withdrawn all his funds in the Bank of England. His brokerage accounts, everything, it seems."

"Why would he?"

"To have it with him, so he could keep an eye on it?" Philip ventured.

Quiggs sat down behind the desk, his face bleached. "He did not tell me, but I knew he was distressed this last month or so. He had a partner, or a contact, who he suspected was out to swindle him. I believe it was Lord Cameron. The day he died, he was most upset, hastily wrote several letters, and I mailed them."

"To whom were they addressed?" Philip asked.

The man passed a hand over his face. "Individuals. One was to Regent Street, number forty-two. I did not note the name. Another went to his club, White's, to be held for a Mister M. Smith, and the last was sent to Jacques's, his tailor's establishment."

Philip took up the pen and wrote the details on a scrap of paper.

Quiggs held out the key. "Please take this, Miss Fiona. I cannot be responsible for this sum of money. It is too much, too much."

"Be easy, Quiggs," she kindly said, "you have done well. We will sort this out. Meantime, do not go anywhere. Keep your place here. Are you owed your salary?"

"Not until the month's end."

"If you require more, come to me. I seem to be rich." She closed the safe and turned the key. Back went the plaque. "Unless it all belongs to someone else. But who?"

Philip strolled around the room. He would track down those addresses. See who turned up when he knocked on the door. He glanced again at the coffin, which was lying crooked on the table. Bracing himself for the weight, he pushed to get it even. But it moved half a foot, threatening to tip over. He quickly moved it back, and it had no weight!

"Quiggs, lend a hand here."

The fellow stepped closer. Philip pondered what

the hell to say. "Fiona, I um, I need to open this and look in."

She jumped. "Whaaaat?"

"Come here, please." She edged over, her expression cautious. He gave the coffin a small push. It slid. "Something is wrong here. I need to look inside."

She stared at the coffin. "The lid was open before." Then she stepped way back and covered her eyes. "Go ahead."

Philip and Quiggs turned the bolts top and bottom at either side, and slowly lifted the lid.

"Holy salvation," Quiggs mumbled.

Fiona peeped around her hands.

The coffin was empty.

Fiona gaped, astonished. Folds of satin padding, but nothing else. "Where is he?" she muttered.

"My word," Quiggs whispered.

They all stood there, bewildered.

"Cameron!" Philip exclaimed. "I wager he is behind this. Quiggs, you have that paper from the bank stating the will must be read?"

"Yes, sir." He patted his coat pocket. "Right here. The funds cannot be released until then."

"Well, but—" Fiona tried to think. Her brain revolved in her head.

"If there is no death, why read a will?" Philip explained. "With no corpse, Cameron can allege fraud and claim what he says is owed. Ten thousand pounds."

"He shall not have it!" she cried. "He cannot get away with stealing a dead person!"

"They came right in the open windows," Philip reasoned. "Likely after Cameron checked the bank accounts. What a tactic."

A tap at the door. They all froze.

"Yes?" Fiona called.

"Mr. Frisk has arrived, Miss Fiona."

"Please show him into the drawing room, Sumpter. I shall be right along." She dropped the key into a bottom desk drawer and turned to the men. "I will keep him occupied. In the meantime, I suggest you put whatever weight you can find in the coffin and close it tight."

"Eh?" murmured Quiggs.

"Capital idea!" Philip enthused. "Quiggs, what here is unnecessary?"

The man glanced around. Fiona went out the door and shut it, nearly falling over the ghastly wreath. She smoothed her hair, trotted to the drawing room, her pulse beating in her throat, and went in.

"Mr. Frisk," she greeted the florid man. "So good of you to come and be of aid in such a trying time."

He bowed. "Not at all, Miss Seymour. I am pleased to serve you."

"Do sit down, sir. I need to catch my breath." She sank into a chair, aiming to appear mournful. "Such a dark task. But you must see such losses every day. How fine of you to carry on."

"Oh, yes," he said, taking a seat. "One learns to deal with the natural, if difficult, processes of life. Like the fairest blossoms, we only have our little span of days. Thoughtful arrangements and a care for tradition and correctness help us along the path, and we do what must be done."

"I am so relieved we called on you, Mr. Frisk. Everything has been, ah, just as it should be."

"Yes, indeed," Frisk bragged. "I take pride in my

work, ma'am." He brought forth a large pocket watch. "My men await your pleasure, Miss Seymour. At your command, we will be on our way."

Fiona thought of fainting, to delay this, but was saved when Quiggs and Philip strolled in.

"Ah, Mr. Frisk," Philip said with a smile. "Has the hour come round?"

"Yes, sir. It is just on two of the clock."

"I will get my things," Fiona added. "One minute, please."

Frisk and Quiggs exchanged greetings as Fiona dashed up the stairs to her room. The yellow gown! Most unsuitable, but she had no time to change. To complete this unseemly ensemble, she added a straw hat with a trailing red ribbon. Gazed in the foggy glass, gave up, clutched her gloves and reticule, and rushed out again. She descended to the foyer as four men came from the library carrying the coffin, the wreath on top. They stepped solemnly down the hall, and Fiona was overtaken by a deluge of mixed emotions.

Philip appeared at her side, and she leaned against him. The procession moved out the door and down the walk, the coffin balanced on the men's shoulders. Jem was on the box of her carriage, and Walsh waited by the door.

The coffin was placed in the back of a glass-enclosed hearse, led by two black horses with feathery black harness plumes that fluttered in the light breeze. The sun shone down on the empty street. Walsh helped her into her carriage, Philip followed, and Quiggs joined them. In moments, the vehicles pulled away and slowly proceeded toward Park Lane.

It was all incredible, Fiona thought, all of it. Philip

took her gloved hand, and she felt his warmth. She glanced across to Quiggs, whose attentive countenance suggested he was not unhappy to be a daredevil. As for Philip, well, he was extra wonderful.

"Thank you both," she said, and meant it. "For everything." Then she sat back and relaxed. Save your energy, she told herself. This adventure was not yet done.

The journey to Heavenly Repose Cemetery was not long. This turned out to be a triangle of open land tucked behind an aged clapboard church, now an office of the Church of England. Nonetheless, the stained glass in the windows dappled the plots with reflections of rose, gold, and blue. Philip considered it as good a place as any for a final rest. The viscount however, had not yet arrived, in more ways than one.

The hearse stopped along a grassy lane, and the carriage halted. The pallbearers alighted and busied about removing the coffin. Frisk hurried to and fro, inspecting the open grave and conversing with workers standing a short distance away. Back he came.

"All is correct, Miss Seymour. I will see to it all."

She adjusted her hat, mindful of her yellow gown. "I do not wish to stay in the carriage."

"But miss, it is not considered—"

"No one is here to judge me. And I would pay my respects to my mother."

Frisk reluctantly handed Fiona down, and Philip followed, admiring her courage. The gravesite was several rows in. The open plot was adjacent to a grave with a small white stone engraved with *Viscountess Eleanora Seymour 1775-1805.* No sentiment. A metal urn fixed atop the stone contained dead rosebuds.

Fiona stooped and picked out the faded blooms. "I come often," she quietly said.

Philip did not intrude, but it was a damned poor showing. No friends or family, no vicar, no fresh flowers, just that obnoxious wreath. He would like to spin it across the property like a wheel, over the uneven, motley bunch of markers.

The pallbearers did their job. The coffin was placed on ropes and lowered into the earth without ceremony or comment. Poor Fiona appeared distraught. Maybe for her mother, since the departed was not in attendance but stashed somewhere like a cask of ale. Maybe in the river, Philip mused. Impossible to keep him around; days had gone by. He would be ripening by this time, and the thought that Cameron would have to deal with it was cheering.

Frisk nodded, gratified as Fiona tossed in a scoop of soil, and the deed was done. If questioned, the lot of them could testify they did not know the coffin contained books, papers, folders, and a hefty wooden stepstool.

Fiona politely thanked Frisk and even the four pallbearers. A shower of dried petals fell from the dead roses she held. She tossed the stems aside, her face sad.

"Time to go, Fiona," he murmured and took her arm.

Followed by Quiggs, they returned to the carriage. The hearse pulled away, and the two vehicles proceeded back down the lane. At the street, Frisk and companions went one way, and they went another, Fiona clearly unburdened.

"I am so glad you were there, both of you. It was terrible. Even with an empty coffin, it was a funeral, and my father *is* dead, we know. Mercy, when we find him, I must go through it all again."

The dear girl must prepare. "I would not count on finding him, Fiona," Philip said.

"Maybe they did not take him far," she said hopefully. "We did not look in the back garden, or the mews. I realize a dead man cannot easily be—So, they must dispose of him? My God. That would be an atrocity!"

"It could certainly earn them a stretch in prison," he acknowledged.

Quiggs agreed. "Without doubt. I would be glad to bear witness that the viscount has been cruelly abducted."

"We must keep silent, Quiggs," Philip warned. "And who would ask? There is a signed death certificate, and the servants know he died. Now we wait. Not for long, I wager. It will be interesting to see Cameron's bloated face, when he learns the ceremony has gone forward."

"He will come," Fiona said gloomily. "The vermin is persistent. We must devise a plan. And what about this marriage contract?"

"That cannot legally stand. We know that, but he does not know we know. You might tentatively agree, but be in distress over the death."

"Can I put him off? What about the mourning period? That would last a year."

"He will attempt to get around that some way," Philip replied, "and want the ceremony performed quickly. But he cannot force you down the aisle, Fiona. If things get tight, say you are already married."

Her green eyes widened. "To whom?"

"To me."

Fiona had thought nothing else could reach her tattered emotions, but this was a fresh blow. The astonishing man contrived a plan for every situation!

"We need to find out more, Fiona," he insisted.

Quiggs was listening. She did not know what to do. Philip moved closer to her. Oh, those mocking eyes!

"A special license would have us married in a trice, my dear."

"Oh, how divinely romantic. And then what? Besides, I do not wish to marry. I would like to do what I please, after a life of my father and his maneuvering. I deserve to be myself for once and not be dangled before the whole city like an ornament. And I am done with the ton. I never wish to go back to dancing with men I do not even care to talk to."

Quiggs grinned, pleased by this attitude, which surprised her. Philip just smiled knowingly, and she wanted to smack him. They reached home, she dismissed Jem and Walsh, and the three entered the house to find a worried Sumpter.

"All went well, Miss Fiona?" he quietly asked.

"Yes, Sumpter, it did. Please have a full tea sent to the drawing room, if you will."

"Right away, miss."

She left her hat and gloves on the hall table and suddenly tired, would be glad to find a chair.

Quiggs bowed. "I will go to the library, Miss Fiona, and straighten up."

"Come and have refreshments, Quiggs. It has been quite a day. The library can wait."

The men followed her to the drawing room. She sank onto the tapestry sofa and warmed herself before the fire. Philip sat beside her, and Quiggs took a chair.

"Where is the will, Quiggs?" she asked.

"In the safe, miss. Under all that money."

"I am interested to see it. Likely, I have been excluded."

"It was last signed and notarized first of January 1815," he added. "I did not read it."

"No telling what it says. Or what there was to leave. What did he intend to do with the swag?"

"Swag." Philip laughed.

"Might it be stolen?" she asked.

"From whom?"

"Perhaps," she suggested, "he meant to leave England with it and defy his creditors. Namely Cameron. But how can we believe anything that man says? The whole affair is a muddle."

"He could not travel with such a cargo of loot," Philip said. "It would need to be converted to bearer bonds or some such."

"But he ran out of time," Quiggs put in.

"Yes, he did. Or was he going to pass it on to someone?"

They pondered this as tea was brought in by Daisy. The maid placed the tray on the low table.

"Thank you, Daisy. All is well in the kitchens?"

"Yes, miss. Cook is preparing a fine joint. We are all relieved the event is over."

Funeral meats, she thought. "Yes. We will go on, Daisy, and find our way together."

"Thank you, miss," the maid said and left the room.

Fiona filled cups. Philip and Quiggs helped themselves to small sandwiches and the iced cakes. She had done her best to reassure everyone, to present firm confidence, but she was frightened. A worried place in her breast could not be soothed. Her home might be taken away, and she would be cast onto the streets. Her friendships amounted to nothing; the ton offered no refuge. Cameron would come and force her away from what little she could count on. She lifted her cup and her hand shook. Oh, God, what would happen to her?

"I will not let you down, Fiona," Philip said. "I promise to stay close by, until all this is settled."

Quiggs put down his cup. "If I may have the key, Miss Fiona, I will take care of the post."

"Oh. I put it in the bottom desk drawer, on the left."

"I will be in the library, if wanted." Quiggs took his leave.

Philip put his arm about her shoulders. "Fiona, I must go home and check my mail."

She felt ill.

"Come with me. We will stay together. I do not want you alone in the house."

"Please," she whispered. "I fear Cameron will come."

"He will, and I want to be here when he shows up. We can be back in good time for dinner."

They stood and strolled to the foyer. Fiona took up her hat and gloves.

"Sumpter, tell Quiggs we will return shortly."

"Very good, miss."

Philip put on his hat, and they went out the door. Fiona glanced anxiously about as they reached the street. He took her arm. "No one will ever again threaten or hurt you, sweetheart. I swear it."

Once again, Fiona believed him. A person had to believe in something to have hope. She was more than willing to put her trust in Philip Laughton.

Chapter Six

They covered the short distance, Fiona on his arm. Philip was sharply aware of her distress, but the girl had grit. Whatever happened, she remained steadfast, moving in whatever direction opened up. With a woman like her beside him, he could attempt anything.

A carriage was parked in front of his residence. Too late, he realized Fiona did not yet know all. Nothing for it, up the steps they went, and he dropped the knocker. The butler answered, his suspicious glance directed to Fiona.

"Sir," he whispered. "You have a caller. I put him in the sitting room and offered brandy."

"Very good, Reston. This is Miss Seymour."

"Ma'am," he said, with a bow.

"Mr. Reston," she sweetly answered.

This pleased the old boy, and he led them to the room. As Philip had anticipated, it was Malrose, toasting himself in an armchair before the fire. He directed an appreciative gaze Fiona's way.

"Good afternoon," he said, not rising.

"Greetings. May I introduce Miss Fiona Seymour? Fiona, this gentleman is my superior."

"How do you do, sir?"

"Ma'am, I am honored."

"Take a seat, Fiona. Let me begin, Malrose. You got my note?"

"I did. It confirmed suspicions."

"There is more to relate. Viscount Greathouse, Miss Seymour's father, died unexpectedly two days ago. Cameron and the man had struck a deal. The viscount signed a marriage contract without Fiona's consent, since Cameron reputedly holds the viscount's considerable debts. Fiona refused the man, and the father was soon dead, leaving the matter in the air. Cameron demands the contract be honored."

"Nonsense," Malrose muttered.

"Yes, but Cameron does not know Fiona is aware of this." Philip saw the girl was taking this in stride and went on. "As I informed you, I believe Cameron is the third man in the, um, French matter. And the viscount may have been involved in some way."

"What French matter?" Fiona asked.

"Wait one moment, my dear." Philip continued, "We had the Greathouse accounts at the Bank of England frozen until the will is read, preventing Cameron from realizing ten thousand pounds held in the viscount's name. It was scheduled to be paid to Cameron's account today."

Malrose nodded. "Well done."

"But the complications go on. Just before the funeral today, we discovered the dead man's body had been taken, leaving behind an empty coffin. With no corpse, Cameron, we think, would assert there was no legitimate death. Therefore, nothing would be in his way to claim the money and likely, pass it on to the French. However, we did not make a scene. This afternoon, the empty coffin, weighted with debris, was buried."

"I say!" Malrose exclaimed.

"Now we intend to wait until a flummoxed Cameron shows up. In addition, three letters were mailed in haste, according to Viscount Greathouse's secretary, Quiggs. We have taken him into our confidence. He is a good man." Philip handed Malrose the scrap of paper. "No name on the Regent Street address, but the others are clearly directed."

"Excellent. I will have these checked."

"One more thing, Malrose. When a wall safe was opened in Greathouse's library, it was stuffed with cash. More than we could count. Gold coins, stacks of currency, and who knows what else. Where exactly the monies came from or were going, Quiggs could not say. He was as surprised as we were."

Malrose thought this over, rubbing his chin with his good hand.

"I am glad to help," Fiona said, "if you will advise me. Cameron will return, I know. He thinks I will marry him because I am penniless." She paused. "Is he a traitor? Was my father?"

"I have received no information regarding your father, Miss Seymour," Malrose answered. "But we now know Cameron is funneling money to France in some way." He shifted in his chair. "I too, have news. Lord Meacham was found dead this morning, in an alley off Piccadilly, stabbed in the heart."

"Why, I know him!" Fiona cried. "I have often seen him at ton gatherings. Dead!"

"Ah," Philip breathed. "He was a talky drunk."

"Outlived his usefulness, I wager," Malrose opined.

"Well, whatever is all this about?" Fiona inquired.

"Murderous treachery, Miss Seymour, but we are

on their trail. Colbourne has done heroic work, many times risking everything to bring vital information home to England."

"Who is Colbourne?" she asked.

Philip did not answer.

Malrose lifted himself from his chair and took up a cane with a fox head grip. "I must go and see to these matters. Keep in touch, my friend. Delighted to meet you, Miss Seymour." He hobbled away to the door, and Reston let him out.

"Who is Lord Colbourne?" Fiona repeated.

"Well," Philip began, "that is…uh, I am."

"You have a *title*?" she whispered.

"Yes, but—"

She took up a cushion and struck him with it. "You scandalous rascal, have you done anything but lie?"

He dodged more blows. "Let me explain…ow!" He grabbed her hands, and she tried to kick him. "Dammit, I was trying to—ouch, quit! I had to keep my secrets."

She threw the cushion across the room. "Dastardly villain! Toying with me. Pretending to like me. You only wanted t-to find out about my father, blast you!"

Philip got a grip on her. "I do not know beans about your father. I wanted to find the traitors who sent that cutter after me. Cameron was one of them. So was Meacham, but he had a loose tongue, and they killed him for it. These are dangerous men, Fiona. How could I tell you more?"

She made to rise, her green eyes full of fire. Philip pulled her down onto his lap. She tried to bite his hand.

"What a woman," he said, hanging onto her. "I never want to lose you, Fiona. I worship and adore you."

"You will say anything. The supposed title is a fraud for your spying. So-called my lord, you are a viscount? Just like my father. Pardon me, my lord. That is why you did not go sailing about on someone else's boat? Shameful, to play at war."

He wanted to shake her. "Playing? I lost three good men, and my fine ship!"

"It all seems bogus to me. I want to go home. It is time for my dinner. If Cameron comes, I will give him a hug and a kiss for you and sing *La Marseillaise*." She waved a hand. "*Allons, enfants*—" she warbled.

"A deplorable accent, my girl. I will be there, and let me say, I am not a viscount."

Fiona held her head. "So! That is a sham, too?"

He had enough of this. "I am for now, at least, the ninth Earl of Colbourne."

She attempted to twist his ear. Philip evaded.

"Ohhhhh," she yelped, "I will hate you forever!"

He dumped her off his lap. "Let us go. I am starving. Reston!"

The butler scurried in. "Yes, my lord?"

"I am out for the evening. Did Pearce arrive?"

"He did, sir. He is seeing to your garments."

"Very good. Back later."

Philip invited a reluctant Fiona to take his hand, but she would not. Instead, she floated out the front door like she was on ice, and he followed. *Damn her*, he crossly mused, *she is splendid. Wait until she finds out who I am now.*

Fiona marched home, full of anger. No one told her anything. She was shunted off as undeserving, just a female, not worth anyone's confidences. Her father had told her nothing, never shared an informative conversation. Quiggs had not said a living word for years, just watched her come and go. She was little more than a servant, except she had no work. No *occupation*, as Father had chided. Blast them all.

She glanced up at Philip. He was no better, except he liked to kiss her. Give her little squeezes, and she had fallen for it. Smooth as glass, this sailor. Full of love words. She had been too ignorant to see it, so starved as she was for affection. It made her blood boil. Fiona felt robbed of a fragile dream, one she had yearned to nourish, and it was too much to bear.

They reached the house. Fiona did not go up to the porch but continued on around the property to the back garden and through the garden gate. She went on to the rosebushes and the shrubbery and peered carefully underneath them, but the garden was empty and dark. No trace of Father, nor was he in the mews or stable yard.

"He is not here, Fiona," Philip whispered.

She turned back toward the house. "I had to see." She retraced her steps, searching all around, both disappointed and relieved. What if he had been there? Then what? He would be in rather poor shape by this time. The thought made her woozy. God above.

The butler let them in.

"Did anyone call, Sumpter?" she asked.

"No, Miss Fiona. Quiggs took his leave saying he would return tomorrow around noon. He left this key."

She took it. "Thank you. Well, um, we will be in the drawing room." Sumpter opened the doors, and she went in, Philip on her heels. She felt wound tight as the hall clock and collapsed on the settee.

"Let us have a brandy," Philip suggested.

"Certainly."

He poured from the decanter and handed her a glass. Fiona took a big drink and gagged. She fought to swallow, and down it went with a bubble of air. It burned like fire, scorching her throat and all the way to her stomach. Her face and neck heated, and she burped.

"You are supposed to sip."

She put down the glass. "Why? It was revolting."

"You were not permitted liquor?" he asked.

"I was not permitted anything Father wanted." She eyed him. He had fooled her by being so winsome and sounding sincere. "Do I call you something else now? One of your titles?"

"Philip will do."

"Not proper; once again I fail. But it is too late for proprieties. I am ruined." She giggled. "Cameron will not want me now."

"Yes, he will."

"But I may be a social disgrace," she claimed, "if I was seen at the Featherstones' ball, or going about, unchaperoned, with you. He wanted to show me off to the ton like a prize horse. And you and I have kissed. Repeatedly."

"Kissing has not damaged your virtue, Fiona."

"Cameron might think so." She studied the brass key. "I will take all that money and leave England. Go to Italy, perhaps. The weather there is very fine, I have heard, and women are treated with respect. I have read novels which stated this fact."

"Which ones?"

Fiona recalled he had attended Oxford and became vague. "Several. Also, I have read *Moll Flanders*."

He had the audacity to laugh. "Scarcely a treatise

on women's rights."

"She made bad choices, but poor Moll was alone and afraid. Never mind all that. I consider myself a capable person. I just have had little experience of the world." She sighed. "I imagine I am going to find out more about everything."

"I can teach you," Philip murmured, edging closer on the settee.

Fiona edged away. "I have also read *Tom Jones*. You remind me of him. He was passionate but had no more sense than Moll. And he was, to some excess, um, a lover of women."

"You find fault with this? You like to be loved."

"Yes, I have found this out. How many others have you taught?"

"None. All the intriguing women I have known had seen the balloon go up."

She scowled. "Pardon?"

A tap at the door, and the butler entered. "Miss Fiona, dinner is served."

"Thank you, Sumpter. Come to my humble table, if it pleases you, my possible lord."

Philip put his long arm around her. "Give me a kiss first."

She stifled a laugh. "Do you want your food to cool?"

"My ardor will heat it up again."

He gave her a sound, lingering kiss. Her senses reeled as next, he lifted her to her feet. Fiona ambled to the doors at his side, in deeper with this mystery man than she was before.

****

Philip partook of a fine loin chop and a selection of

delicious vegetable dishes, artfully prepared. Fiona pushed her food around her plate, ate a bite, then pushed it around again.

He buttered a yeast roll and chewed. What was he going to do about this bold female? She was ready to charge out into the world. Which orb, he feared, was not quite prepared for a devastating mix of nymph and siren. It had gotten to the point that her faint, feminine scent gave him the shakes. The girl presented a tremendous temptation, which he must not yield to.

He should immediately stop kissing her. Every time he did, his willpower slipped away like frightened water. He had gotten into this predicament without sufficient consideration. Over she went on the sidewalk, and he should have gone on his way. But, both intrigued and lonely, he had decided to take her home and tumble her into his bed. That had not worked out, and those damn letters had torn a hole in his heart. Then the drama began.

The result of it all was he had a burning desire to love Fiona up, down, and sidelong until she said everything he wanted to hear. What exactly that was, Philip did not bother to examine. He just longed for every intimacy she would allow, aching to devour her like candy. He sipped the excellent Burgundy. Because she was beautiful, sweet, naïve, clean, and a virgin if he ever encountered one. Off limits. Forbidden. Unless he meant to marry her. Which he decidedly did not.

The endless war blocked the way, for one, plus Malrose and his schemes. Now that the man had him on a string, he might never escape. He had three months, then he would have to go back at it. He would help clear out this current rat's nest of traitors, then head for

Hampshire and home. Rest. Forget. He had no time to spare for Miss Seymour.

Ah, dessert. A light claret and a vanilla sponge ended the meal, and Philip was well satisfied.

Fiona watched Philip from the corner of her eye. He was a big man, she noted for the tenth time. Classic Norman head, wide shoulders, long arms, large hands. She imagined those hands on her, exploring her person. It made a shaky tremble in her middle.

Gregg fussed over him, offering more wine, and another slice of cake. Daisy hovered, ready to please. It annoyed Fiona that he was sitting in her father's chair. She should be sitting there. *She* was the head of the house now.

"An excellent meal, Fiona."

"Another occasion when you have been narrowly saved from starvation," she drily remarked.

"I like to eat. You, my friend, ate a good deal of nothing tonight."

"I had enough. Gregg, coffee in the drawing room, please. And thank you both for the dinner. Tell Cook the sponge was perfect."

"Yes, miss," Daisy replied. "I will say so."

They strolled there and sat down on the familiar tapestry sofa, facing the fire. It crackled and spit, a log fell, and Fiona worried for the future. Would Cameron take everything? Would she be friendless and destitute? Whose money was that in the safe? Why had Cameron said he held father's debts? If he did, where did the cache of money come from? What about her five hundred pounds plus interest? She would subtract that amount promptly, whomever the cash belonged to.

Philip nudged her arm. "Fiona, stop fretting."

"It is very troubling that nothing has been settled! Where is my father? Cameron, the money—it is all suspended in the air. Time drags, and then speeds up, and everything is a tangle."

He leaned toward her. "You have lovely skin, Fiona, sweetheart." He dragged a warm thumb down her cheek. "And your lips are the color of a pink tulip. When I kiss them, they taste of spring, fresh and new."

He gathered her up like she had no substance. Fiona did not speak and gazed into his eyes, only inches away. Dark, melty, brandy brown, they said things to her, they beckoned.

"I would like to take your hair down," he murmured, "and see it all spill down your fabulous skin."

Scandalous! "Now?" she whispered.

"Well, someday. Then I would take off that little gown you have on. Are you wearing those satin stays?"

"N-no!"

"So much the better."

A tap and Daisy entered with the coffee tray.

A respite. "Thank you, Daisy. I will pour."

"Yes, miss."

Fiona filled a cup and handed it to him, poured for herself, added a sugar lump and a splash of cream, and waited for what exciting things he would say next.

"Then," he went on, "I would make love to you for hours. Maybe for days."

Fiona conquered a blush and haughtily sipped her coffee. She must stay above this banter. "You are playing with me, Philip. Trying to shock me."

"Oh, I believe it would take a great deal to shock you, Fiona. You have a clear eye and take what comes."

He touched the fabric of her skirt. "Most remarkable for someone not quite grown up."

"I will soon be twenty."

"Eh? You were only just nineteen. Old age threatens?"

She pulled her skirt away. "How madly arrogant, Philip. You think you know everything. And should you be saying such dodgy things to me? Is that done in your maritime circles? Or are you just practicing, for when you meet women of your rank?"

"I am saying what I think, what I feel."

"You have been too long at sea and have lost your perspective. And since I am of no consequence, you feel free to kiss me with abandon."

"You have not seen any abandon, girl, not yet." He sat closer. "You are of great consequence to me, Fiona. You have turned me all around."

"I should not wonder," she blurted. "Threats of social ruin, dead men, wads of cash, spies and traitors. And you were gravely ill and your ship and crew lost. You may not know what you are saying." She paused to catch her breath. "So, I must forget it."

"Then I will start all over. And I have recovered. The Colbournes are made of sturdy stuff."

"Oh, I am sure. For centuries, no doubt. How long have you been titled? If you are?"

"Since I was seventeen."

"Mercy, what happened?"

"My father was in the diplomatic service, stationed in Lisbon. My mother joined him for a short holiday, and they both contracted cholera."

"Ohhh, how awful."

"I was able to finish up my studies and went home

129

to Hampshire to run the estate. Four years ago, I left the property in good hands and took up my war duties."

"I am most touched, Philip."

"But you lost your mother at nine, when just a babe."

"There is no way to measure pain and loss. It was all difficult, especially since my father was mean and dismissive. But you had a harder way, to lose both parents at once."

"Very generous of you. I got by."

Her eyes filled in tearful sympathy. "I am so sorry, nonetheless."

Back he came, closer than before. "What a tender girl you are, Fiona. It gladdens my heart."

"Oh, well. I feel very sad for my troubles, so I understand other people's. If I learn of them, that is, if they say. I have come to realize how little real talk goes on. It is nonsense, most of the time. Gossip and the latest scandal. All the while, everyone wants a true friend they can speak to about what is important."

He agreed. "People hide themselves."

"Life as a masked ball," she mused. "But masks are taken off at midnight."

"If midnight comes." He gazed into her eyes. "Let us not wait to speak."

"Oh, good. You first."

Philip smiled handsomely. "In three days, Fiona, you have captured my heart."

"Balderdash," she complained. "You are not playing fair. You must speak the *truth*."

"I have."

Now he had done it. A wall went up between them. Her green eyes snapped.

"I must object. You go too far, Philip. I know you are only entertaining yourself. A sailor on leave, shall we say?" She clasped her hands together in front of her breast, as if to hold him off. "I mean, you have been enormous help to me, honestly, and we have enjoyed, um, we have—"

"Do not tell me what has gone on, Fiona. I know what I have said, and what I have done. Kissing and holding you was not wasting time. I meant it. What were you doing?"

Those eyes widened. How guileless. "Ho, ho!" he teased. "Let us have some of that real talk, m'dear."

She defiantly raised her chin, the vixen. "As I said, I enjoyed it. Every single bit. Your kisses, the way you smell, your clothes. Your male everything. I wanted it all, but I have been under no illusions. You are footloose, and maybe, just maybe, titled, and I am at a considerable disadvantage. Possibly penniless, my reputation in doubt, no family, friends, or powerful connections. So you are dallying, and I am so longing for affection, I soak it up. I know I am absurd, but there you are. In one more day, you will be gone back to Hampstead and forget me."

"Hampshire."

"Right."

"Kiss me, Fiona."

"Ohhhh," she mourned, "how long are you going to go on with this?"

He leaned back. "Another day or two may see developments. My mind is on Cameron and his next move. I am waiting for him to come. We outwitted him today with the false burial, but he is after that money, and he is after you."

"The money at the bank?"

"That, and the monies in the wall safe. I think Cameron may know your father was holding out on him, and I believe he was. What about that kiss?"

"Philip—"

"The world is a barren place, Fiona, for a man alone. Would you believe I knew no women in the last four years?"

"No."

"Well, it is mostly true." He studied his nails. "More like three and a half years. Of course, there was that time two years ago, and a remarkable incident on my last birthday."

Fiona frowned, disturbing the freckles on her nose. He held her nearer.

"The truth is, I have only kissed you. It was worth the wait."

"What a fable, sir."

"Did Cameron touch you, Fiona?"

Startled, she cried, "Certainly not!"

"No one else claimed a kiss?"

She pushed at her lovely hair. "Oh, about a dozen of them," she airily replied. "Rash lads, whom I fascinated. They could not restrain themselves. I was forced to endure their damp clutches."

He laughed heartily.

"You think you have all the secrets, Philip," Fiona insisted, "but I have mine."

"I wager you do. I would like to have a look at them, then take a big bite. Nibble and lick every part of you."

She gave him a push. "Stop! Do not say these things. I have never *heard* of such. It is because you defy rules, that is what. You sneak back and forth across the channel in the dark and think terrible thoughts. Keeping it all pent up may have affected your reason."

"Well, obviously I was not adequately sneaky. I did not feel 'pent up,' as you term it, until you took that facer on the sidewalk. Since then, I am pent up as hell."

She absently touched her forehead. "I was upset and stumbled. I would have been all right."

"Your eyes rolled around like dried peas, you staggered drunkenly, and a crowd formed. I saved you from public disgrace."

She sniffed. "Thank you so much."

"What gratitude," he growled. "Next time, I will not trouble myself."

"Next time, I will watch my step and not fall in with rowdy sailors."

Then she smiled, and his heart lurched.

"Was that real talk?" she asked.

"Absolutely." Philip kissed her before she could resist. Too luscious. She invaded his every cell and sinew. Pent up? If he did not make love to her soon, he would disintegrate. He has been ill, was in a weakened condition and needed her help.

"Fiona, love," he whispered. "I ache for you."

She blinked. "For my problems?"

"No, woman, for your body."

She laughed merrily. "What fun. We must always speak directly."

"God above," Philip groaned. "I am conversing with an infant."

"Ah, such a man of the world. You have seen it all, at least as far as Calais. Bobbing over the sea like a cork."

"Make light, you heathen girl. It was bloody life and death. I sweated in fear of being blown to smithereens for four long years, and it finally happened. Three good men went down at the last, and not one of them had reached the age of forty. The ship was on fire, taking on water fast, I nearly drowned! Do you think it was a lark? Ha! You were dancing at balls, eating delicacies, and flaunting yourself."

"Flaunting!" she cried, insulted. "I was under great duress."

"You could have refused!"

"Oh, could I? You have no idea how it is to have no resources, no way out, to be bullied, deprived, and browbeaten. I depended on that five hundred pounds to get away, find my freedom, and he stole it. If he had not died, I would be married to that little pig Cameron."

They glared at each other.

"So. You are a hero, Philip, and I am nothing in comparison, but weak and spineless."

He lifted her hand and kissed it. "I am a pitiable fellow, to quarrel with an angel. I knew what I was getting into out there in the dark, doing my duty. Forgive me."

"No, no, forgive me, Philip," she gently said. "I know what you endured. Truly I do. I was under no hardship, just sort of mashed. My feelings, my hopes for my life, did not count. I felt imprisoned and worth no better."

"You are worth a kingdom, Fiona, darling woman."

They embraced. Each of them had suffered, Philip knew. No one would ever hurt her again, he vowed, or diminish her value, when she was so fine. He would see to it, God willing. The war would wait for three months to have another go at him. Sadly, he thought, holding Fiona close, it seemed the war would never end.

They sat together, talking, warmed by the fire and by the closeness, and Fiona was happy. Just being with Philip made the whole world a more optimistic place. How fortunate she had been to meet him and bask in the security of his presence. He would go away, of course, but now she knew what was possible, if you found someone who understood what you were about. Now she would look in the right places. Wherever those were. Not among the ton and its starched frivolities. Nothing at all was there.

The truth of it was Fiona did not want Philip to ever go away. She wanted *him*, not some murky stranger. This idea fell right into place. He would stay, and they could be together. Did he not say—she blushed despite herself—that he wished to make love to her? How could she keep that going? In fact, increase his interest?

She must be audacious and outlined a strategy. Fiona leaned against him languidly and put her hand on his knee. This was rather a stretch, his legs were so long. She inched up his thigh, a rock of muscle. Maybe he was unaware. Best say something.

"You are a very appealing man, Philip."

"Hmmm."

"I imagine women find you very attractive. I do, you know."

He cut a glance her way. "Do you, now?"

Fiona moved her hand up to his coat and the pretty buttons. "I like being near you and enjoy the things you do."

"What things?" he asked. "When I touch you? When I kiss you? Would you like more?"

She hesitated.

"Now you are playing with *me*, Fiona."

"Well, I am trying to er, increase your interest. I do not quite know how to do that." She took a steadying breath. "What more, exactly?"

He looked right into her eyes and put his enormous hand on her breast! This led to a tumult of outrage and hot, wanton sensations. She fought off the impulse to bash him for extreme impertinence. Instead, she went limp with delirious enjoyment. Then he kissed her lips and squeezed! Fiona thought she would swoon. Her entire body went into a tremor.

Philip hugged her. "Fiona, you enchantress," he whispered in her ear.

Her mouth dried, preventing an answer. She swallowed.

"I could show you the stars, dear heart, up close." He leaned away. "However, you are not ready."

"How rude!" she cried.

"I do not go about deflowering innocents."

"Well! How innocent do you think I am?"

He scoffed imperially, "Please."

"I will have you know"—she rapidly invented a situation—"that I have a past."

"You have not lived long enough to have a past."

"An outlandish presumption. I could tell you, but it is too private. If you have no interest in me, others do. Have done, that is. Will in the future."

He gazed at the fire. "Rubbish, girl."

"People who lie do not believe others," she

accused.

He faced her, his eyes dark as coffee. "I have not lied."

"Yes, you have, by omission. You did not tell me who you really are."

"That is not all I have not told you, you goose. Was I to lay my whole life before you?"

"Why not? You have certainly invaded mine."

He frowned. "Damn, Fiona, stop taunting me. I am tired of waiting while you strut your stuff. Where is your room?"

"My *r-room*?"

"What is your game?" he demanded. "Are you offering yourself to me, or fooling around?"

Oh, dear. "I am just trying to make you stay. If you go away, I will be…um, so I wanted to ensure your continuing presence."

"Keep it up, and you will get my complete presence. If you catch my meaning." He ran his hand through his longish hair. "I must go home and get some sleep."

"Oh," she yelped, "have I spoiled things between us?"

"No, I am tired. Remember I have been ill."

"I am sooooo sorry. Let me say that you have become important to me. Not because I have all these worries, but because you are, you have been—"

He slipped away from her and stood. "Come along and see me to the door." He lifted her to her feet and pressed her against him. "Think it all over carefully, Fiona, because if you offer yourself, I am likely to accept your considerable gifts. Because I desire you," he added, "with all my being. So take good care."

Fiona enjoyed this delicious threat. They strolled to the doors and to the foyer. Sumpter was elsewhere.

"I will be back early tomorrow. Cameron may be coming, and I want to be here."

"Good. Thank you."

Another smoldering kiss.

"And thank *you*, sweetheart."

Philip opened the door, strode down the walk, and disappeared into darkness. Fiona closed it and threw the bolt. She would think it over, all right. Would she ever. She had seen the outskirts of bliss when he put his hand on her breast, and she longed to see what came next.

****

Philip sauntered home. He was not all that tired, but it had been wise to leave Fiona's arms, lest he succumb and overwhelm the girl on the carpet. She was wildly seductive in the most innocent ways, and it got under his natural reserve. What little he had. He had never been one to hold back when it came to women. Had always considered himself a straightforward man, but when he spoke his mind to Fiona, he was juggling burning coals. The woman was too responsive, for one thing. She represented a sensual abyss, and if he fell in there was no getting out again.

Be rational, he lectured himself. This was a passing infatuation. She was younger than she knows, far too young for him. But how could he leave her to cope with the likes of Cameron? And if not him, somebody else? A unique woman like Fiona would draw every bounder in London. She had certainly drawn him.

After assuming the earldom, Philip had been a conservative young man, mindful of his position, careful of those who might exploit him. This had included females. He had kept his sexual activity out of the light, and never took a virgin. There were always discontented wives and widows, for instance. A lot of them, he had found. He was young and lusty, wealthy, well-formed, and an aristocrat. Then the war had intruded.

Now this Fiona had descended on him like a rich perfume. He had inhaled and become fixed on her. Philip wanted to turn around and go back to Two Twenty and take her upstairs to wherever she stirred the potion that had bewitched him. Cherish her, teach her to love him, and fuck her senseless. Jesus, what a situation.

Reston let him into the house, his expression guarded. "Home safe, my lord. Praise be. Cutthroats and thieves abound in the night, sir."

"There are several out in the daytime, Reston."

"And you are well able to defend yourself, my lord." The butler closed the door and locked it.

Philip saw his relief to shut out danger. "All well here, I trust. I will see you in the morning. Good night."

"Good night, sir."

In his room, his valet, Pearce, waited. Tall, lanky, and dignified in appearance, he was an intelligent man of subtle wit.

"Pearce. Good to see you well."

"And you, sir, to have survived a dunking. Passions ran deep at home to think you at peril."

The man helped him off with his coat.

"I made it by holding on with my teeth. And yourself? Where did Reston find you?"

"In Clapham, at my brother's. A vicar, you may recall, he is contemplating marriage, and it has him prostrate with anxiety."

Philip handed off his neckcloth and pulled his shirt over his head. "On what front? He fears his performance?"

"No, sir, he fears hers. They are a devout couple, which to my mind threatens to quash open, natural feelings. My brother is well cognizant of this fact."

Philip allowed his boots to be removed and shed his breeches and smalls. "No taste of forbidden nectar goads them on?"

"Unhappily not, sir. We are a nation of religion, the mother of manners. Hence, many of us are stultified in our expressions of desire. Not your noble self, I am aware."

"Oh, are you so confident of me, Pearce?"

"Indeed, my lord. I consider you to be free of the social prisons confining the lower orders."

Philip caught the edge of Pearce's smile. He was having him on.

"Not entirely so, Pearce," he replied. "I am at present caught between the rock of propriety and the hard place in my trousers."

Up went Pearce's expressive brows. He pursed his lips and emitted a decorous chuckle.

"I have lately encountered—is there water?"

"Yes, sir."

He sauntered to the dressing room. Pearce filled the bowl, and Philip washed his face and hands. "As I was saying, I have come across a juicy pear, ripe for the picking. But she is young."

"You are young, sir."

"Not that young." He dried off. "The choice is coming. Do I take her and the hell with all else? You have heard about my uncle, Pearce?"

"Yes. God bless him," the valet remarked. "Talk of being young!"

Philip donned his nightshirt. "Uncle was never robust, but only fifty. Fifty, Pearce! I was at sea and late to hear of it. I have signed the papers and taken over the accounts. It is a done thing."

"My condolences, sir."

"It was a shock. I have business here in London, then I will return to Hampshire, and get organized. Become the new me," he muttered, climbing into his bed. "And there is this low-hanging fruit I mentioned. I must deal with her."

"Is she full worth the wanting, sir, if I may inquire?"

He recalled her smile, the freckles, and the feel of her weighty breast. "Yes, Pearce, she is. Good night."

"Good night, sir."

Philip fell into a reverie of taking off Fiona's pretty gown, searching for the satin stays. But she had none on. He was joyous, reached out for her, and fell asleep, a smile on his face.

Chapter Seven

Thursday

Fiona rose early, bathed, dressed, and ate her breakfast in a rush, watching all the while for Philip to arrive. This proved to be silly. It was only eight of the clock when she had finished all this activity. Still, in a jade green muslin gown and white leather slippers, she was confident of her appearance, if nothing else.

She wandered to the drawing room and sat by the front windows. How would she know when he left his bed? She conjured images of Philip rising, exchanging furnishings and bed sizes to suit her notions of how he lived. The man himself was a blur.

If Philip could see her room, he would be appalled. Shabby, mismatched, everything would offend him. Of course, he would not know about the hole in the carpet under her bed. *Where is your room?* he had asked. If she took him there, it had best be dark. Perhaps he can see in the dark, Fiona mused, when he sailed. In a sloop. Odd word, sloop. Slip, slop, sluice.

Why was she thinking these things? She may be losing her mind under the strain of such upheavals. She hastened from the room, down the hall, and out to her garden, filled the copper watering can at the rain barrel and gave her plants a drink. Everything was coming along nicely, but the garden failed to hold her attention and Fiona went back inside.

A knock at the front door! Philip had come. She hurried forward to greet him as Sumpter opened the door.

God in Heaven, it was Cameron! And she had nowhere to hide. Sumpter attempted to deny him entrance, but she intervened. "It is all right, Sumpter, thank you. He may come in for a few minutes."

Cameron bustled in and shouted, "Miss Seymour, I come on official business!" He held out a piece of paper.

Fiona did not take it. He pushed it forward.

"This is a matter of law, therefore you must accept this. It is a subpoena, ordering you to appear at the offices of my solicitor, to adjudicate the signed marriage contract." He wagged the paper at her. "I intend to assert my rights in the matter," he loudly exclaimed, "now that your father is no longer extant."

Fiona smiled at the word extant. "May I see this contract?" she sweetly inquired.

This threw him. "Ah, I do not have it with me, but my solicitor knows of it."

"Mercy, are not solicitors more sedulous as to details? Rather careless of you, your lordship, not to first present your evidence to me. I know little of the law but am an honorable person. If you have an actual claim, prove it to me. Until then, I see no need to respond to your request."

His cheeks puffed out as he stretched to increase his puny stature. "This is insufferable!" he ranted.

"I should say. Sumpter, show the earl out, if you please."

Sumpter, a slight man, nevertheless loomed over

the shorter Cameron, who still had his hat on.

"Time to go, sir," he intoned.

Cameron, looking mad enough to spit, threw the paper to the floor. "I shall return forthwith," he noisily threatened, "with proof!" He stormed out the door and flounced down the walk, his coattails flying.

Sumpter closed the door. Where, Fiona wondered as she retrieved the paper, was Philip?

****

Philip, concealed by the trunk of an elm tree, saw Cameron leave Two Twenty in a hurry, his face red, his boots hardly striking the ground. The man directed his coachman, got in the carriage, and it rolled away.

He crossed the street, went up the walk, and dropped the knocker. Sumpter opened the door cautiously, then beamed. "Mr. Laughton, sir. Good day. Do step in."

"Thank you, Sumpter. How goes it?"

"Eventful, sir. Lord Cameron arrived moments ago and attempted to coerce Miss Fiona. She put him in his place, I assure you."

"Very good. Where is—"

Fiona came down the hallway, his face lovely, her pale green gown flattering, her step light. "Philip." She reached his side. "Welcome."

"Hello, Fiona. How pretty you look. Sumpter informs me Cameron was here."

"Yes. He presented me with this, a subpoena, he said. I would not take it, so he dropped it on the floor."

Philip scanned over the paper, a legal form. "It is a request to appear, not a writ of subpoena. That order comes from a court. You are not legally bound to honor this, Fiona."

"Why should I? There is nothing to be said. I never agreed to the contract, and Father is no longer, ah, extant."

He took her arm; they went to the drawing room and sat down on the gold settee. "It is another threat. If he can persuade you of his claim, he can marry you and thereby get everything. You, the house, and the money."

"I will kill him first," she said, her words quiet, her manner irate.

"He intends to try every trick, thinks he is shrewd and can fool you into believing him. This is a mistake."

"I asked to see the contract, guessing he did not have it with him. Sumpter showed him out the door as he bellowed he would be back with it. Forthwith." She laughed merrily. "I have decided the man is stone deaf. He shouts everything."

Philip shook his head. "What I cannot understand is, with so much at stake, he cannot let loose of his obsession with you."

"Well," Fiona bragged, "I have vast appeal, you know."

He gazed steadily at her. "If he is caught at his schemes, Cameron will hang."

"Then he is truly mad to pursue me."

"He well may be. What sane person would contrive to steal a dead man? Or plot to end the war with their pittance of money? Betray England? No small thing, Fiona, to become a traitor. It makes no sense to me."

"Nor to me. What shall I do when he comes back?"

"Let us go out," he suggested, "and give him an empty house. Delay is still our ally."

"Wonderful. Wait here, and I will get my things."

Fiona dashed away.

Philip sat there, thinking what an ass Cameron was. Driven to get his hands on Fiona and the money in the safe. A thought struck him. Had Greathouse been holding the funds to be transferred to the French? Was that Cameron's frantic motivation? He must pass the loot on, or else? Had he and Harley killed Meacham or had others? Was Cameron in grave danger and becoming increasingly desperate?

Finally, was Fiona's father a traitor? Had he sequestered the money to be sent on to France, or was he a dupe? Philip no longer believed the tale about Greathouse's debts. What Cameron held was the viscount's throat, and the man had bargained away Fiona to satisfy some demand.

It was a coil, to be sure.

****

Fiona chose her best hat, a tan straw trimmed with red silk poppies that perched on her head in a jaunty way. What fun to go out with Philip. Gloves in hand, she hurried back down the stairs as Quiggs arrived. Oh, dear, business must be done.

"Good day, Quiggs," she said in greeting.

"Good day, Miss Fiona. I am returned to see about the matters we discussed."

"Very well. Mr. Laughton is here. I will bring him to the library directly."

The fellow ambled away. Fiona returned to the drawing room. "Quiggs has come. I assume he means to find the will."

"Excellent," Philip said, rising. "Our outing can wait."

Disappointed, Fiona reluctantly followed Philip to

the library. What could the blasted will say that she wanted to hear?

Quiggs took the key from the bottom drawer, swung aside the plaque, and opened the safe. All three of them peered in, but the money and coins were right where they had been. Fiona considered the stacks of cash.

"Before anyone claims this money," she asserted, "I want my five hundred pounds. Plus ten years interest."

Quiggs was thoughtful. "That amount would be in the range of eight hundred pounds."

"Count it out, Quiggs, if you please."

The secretary started peeling bills off the top of a pile. The stack grew, and Fiona felt a grim satisfaction. She had her own back, her nest egg, her stake. It was hers, given to her by Mama. Quiggs put the pile of bills on the desk. Fiona scooped it into the top drawer and closed it.

Now he poked under the money still in the safe, pushed the coin trays aside, and removed two envelopes. "This cash was added recently," Quiggs observed, "and all else went to the bottom."

"Open them, Quiggs," Fiona urged.

He did so and unfolded a paper. "It is the will."

"Oh, mercy," she breathed.

Quiggs sat down in the chair and read. Philip stood by.

Impatient, she asked, "Well, what does it say?"

"It enumerates his accounts at the Bank of England, Threadneedle Street."

The suspense was painful. "What else?"

"The deed to the house is there in a safe box, along

with other family papers. Bequests for the servants in employ are listed, and the like. None of his possessions are entailed." He skimmed down the page. "Here is the last."

"Read it out, Quiggs," Philip said.

" 'All my worldly goods not mentioned above,' " Quiggs uttered solemnly, " 'go to my only daughter, and sole relation, Fiona Mary Clarissa Seymour, on the day of her marriage.' "

"Oh, damn the man," she cried, banging her fist on the desk. "Not tuppence for *me*! It would go to my husband! Robbery, I say, cruel theft of my rights as a person. And what if I choose not to marry? I am to starve?"

"True enough," Philip remarked. "Not to worry, Fiona. Open the other one, Quiggs."

Fiona fumed as he did so. The insult of it, the disregard of her feelings hurt her all over. The mean smallness of her father was a blow to her heart.

"Gads," Quiggs exclaimed. "It is the marriage contract."

Philip bent over the document.

Fiona was amazed. "Well, what a stupid thing," she complained. "Throw it out, Quiggs."

"No, I wish to read it." Philip took it and studied it. "This says Cameron was to give your father five thousand pounds on your wedding day."

She could not reason this out. "But then, what is all *this* money?"

"Mayhap Cameron paid in advance?" Quiggs suggested.

"That cannot be," she objected. "When would he have done so? I never agreed, and we had no acquaintance at all. Well, not enough to hand over five thousand pounds."

"Peculiar," Philip agreed. "And Cameron said he would return with the contract?"

"Yes, he did. I cannot understand what he is about."

"He may have been sounding you out. And the so-called solicitor is likely a cohort." He continued to peruse the document. "This contract is not only signed, it is notarized."

"If he imagines he has paid for me," Fiona hotly stated, "he is wrong!"

"He does not owe the five thousand until you marry. The fool obviously thinks no one is aware of his doings. I am afraid, Fiona, that he believes you have no brains."

"Father told him that. And I keep saying," she maintained, "the idiot does not know me at all. We have seldom spoken. I refused to dance with him. We are total strangers."

"A complex knot," Quiggs murmured.

"We will untangle it," Philip said with confidence. "Quiggs, you are a valuable man. Fiona, give him ten pounds from the safe."

Fiona counted out the bills and handed them to Quiggs.

"What must I do, sir?" he asked.

"Not a thing. It is a well-deserved bonus. Fiona, my dear, where is that famous valise?"

Quiggs, confounded, stared at the bills.

"Upstairs, in the box room," she answered.

"Fetch it, if you will."

She hurried up the flights of stairs. Fiona would

trust Philip to sort this out, but she was no weakling. She would not give up an hour of her freedom to a dunce like Cameron. Back down she went, the valise banging her leg, and to the library. The men were bent over the desk, studying the contract.

Philip opened the case, and Quiggs began to put in the stacks of money, along with the coins. Soon the safe was empty, except for a small notebook, a larger journal, and other business papers.

"Are you going to hide it, Philip?" she asked.

"No, indeed, my dear. We are off to the bank to open an account in your name."

Fiona was thrilled.

Philip worried. The goddamn marriage contract looked tight as a drumhead. Cameron had taken elaborate pains to secure Fiona, no matter her wishes. A sick thing, to pursue a woman that did not want him and try to march over her objections legally. With her father's consent! The whole matter disgusted him. It reeked of bondage.

Fiona dashed about, ordered the carriage, assured Quiggs he could continue on, and spoke to a curvy maid, Daisy.

The carriage arrived, a decent vehicle but nothing special. A young groom jumped to hold the door, and they proceeded down the walk.

"Thank you, Walsh," Fiona said as he helped her in. Philip saw the worshipful look from the lad.

"Yes, Miss Fiona."

He took his seat beside her, and the carriage moved away. There was a long crack in the leather squabs. The girl saw him notice.

"This carriage is old," she said shyly. "Father

would not even consider a new one."

"Still adequate, he thought?"

"Well, too expensive to buy another. Jem, the coachman, patches repairs together. I may as well acknowledge Father was a complete miser."

Philip nodded supportively, so she would say more.

"We have so few servants charwomen must come in. I have never had a lady's maid. Daisy kindly attends me, but she has many other duties. Gregg serves the table and does additional work about the house. And Father bullied them terribly. Not Cook, he valued Mrs. Destin."

They rolled along.

"I hate the house, too, and all the furniture." Then she laughed gaily. "I am picky."

"You have taste, Fiona. Things that do not suit you are a burden."

"I should say! All the furniture in my room are odd pieces from another day. Nothing matches. But I have scads of clothes. Father said my appearance must be beyond reproach. My dressmaker beams when I go there."

"He paid for an ample wardrobe?"

"Yes, so I could look desirable."

"He wasted his money, sweetheart." He laughed. "You would be desirable in nothing at all."

She appeared pleased. "Oh, my. You are wicked, Philip."

"I hope so. Otherwise, how dull I should seem."

Those green eyes shone as she said, "Not you."

Philip considered her carefully. "You would not find me so, in time?"

"Why? You are"—she glanced away—"most

captivating."

"We could perhaps build on that."

Fiona gave him a coquettish smile. "How high?"

He reached out to touch her fair cheek. "To the stars. I know the way."

They reached Threadneedle Street, and the carriage halted before the bank. They glanced out and shared a secret smile.

"The scene of our first encounter," he joked.

Walsh opened the door, and they stepped out. He reached back in for the valise and took her arm.

"Mind your footing, Fiona. There are rough waters."

"I am. This time, we are bringing money *to* the bank. I hope they do not remember me."

They entered the bank, the air scented with currency, and the fellow at the desk rose to greet them. He glanced at Fiona, and Philip saw a flicker of recognition.

"Good day, sir. How may we serve you?"

"This lady wishes to open an account."

"Excellent, sir, ma'am. Will you come this way?"

They followed him to an office. A tall, thin man rose to greet them.

"This is Mr. Chartwell. He handles private accounts."

"Good day. Will you take seats? I believe it is Miss Seymour?" he asked.

"Yes." Fiona said. "I straightened out that other matter, and today I wish to open my own account."

He took a paper from a drawer and a pen from a stand. "In what name?"

"Mine. Fiona Seymour." She watched him write.

"Two Twenty Green Street, London. I will be able to change that address later, should I need to?"

"Yes, ma'am. Just inform us. We will mail a quarterly statement."

She sighed deeply. "Lovely."

"In what amount?" Chartwell asked, his pen poised.

Philip lifted the valise to the desk. "It must be recounted."

Chartwell stood. Philip opened the valise, the man peered in, and stepped back.

"Stiles," he called.

A fellow breezed in. "Yes, sir?"

"Have a teller count this."

The assistant took the valise to an adjoining room. Chartwell's face was a mixture of awe and disbelief. "Might I offer tea," he politely asked, "while we wait?"

****

Fiona was astounded as they left the bank, her new account book tucked in her reticule.

"Mind the sidewalk, Fiona," Philip teased. "I cannot lose you now."

Walsh helped her into the carriage, and Philip followed, Fiona about to fizz over.

"Twenty thousand pounds, Philip! It is beyond belief."

"Not counting the coins, which must be valued. That amount will be added to the balance."

"It is just stunning." She bit her lower lip. "Will I have to give it back?"

"To whom?"

"Yes, there is that. Are we returning home?"

He hesitated for a moment, then said, "I have an

errand, if you would not mind waiting."

"No, it is grand to be out of the house."

Philip rapped on the roof. The panel slid open. "Aye?"

"Doctor's Commons, if you please, Jem."

"Yes, sir." The panel slid shut.

Would he lose respect for her, Fiona wondered? "I would not like you to think I am greedy, Philip, but this is all I have. Maybe forever."

"Forever?"

"Unless I find some work to replenish what I spend. This is what people do, is it not? Unless they have a source of income, something must add to the coffers or they will go empty."

"Coffers," he mused.

"Yes, a strange word. I am sure you have means, as an, um, earl? Sheep and whatnot. Grains."

"My steward is a treasure."

"You are not required to plow fields and so on?" she joked, as the carriage moved forward into traffic.

"Not lately," he answered. "I plowed the waves instead."

They laughed together, Fiona entirely happy. The vehicle traveled on, the streets busy. The air contained the smells of woodsmoke, cut green grass, and the dust of many wheels. Fiona loved London, its crowds and bustle. It was the greatest city in the world. Of course, she had never been anywhere else. She looked at Philip, caught in a ray of sunshine. How beautiful a man. What good fortune to have his company.

"Thank you, Philip, for all you have done for me."

"It was my pleasure, Fiona."

"I would not have known what to do."

"No, you did well all along. As to the death, by the time I arrived, you had absorbed the shock, summoned a doctor, plus jolly Mr. Frisk and the women who prepared the body. Weighty matters to deal with, my dear. Give yourself credit. You have been marvelous."

"Oh," she said, delighted. "Do you think so?"

"You are an exceptional woman. Many would have gone to pieces in a flood of tears. Fallen into a faint and had to apply hartshorn or burnt feathers. No, you went right on like a good soldier."

She thought this over. "Father was not my friend or my ally. It was rather crushing, so I depended on myself."

The carriage entered between a cluster of buildings and at a layby halted. Philip took her hand. "I should not be longer than a quarter of an hour. I see there is a little green space nearby with a bench, if you would prefer to rest there."

"No, thank you. I will wait here. Do take your time."

He leaned to her and lightly kissed her lips. It was so sweet and tender, Fiona wanted to hug him, but he had a task.

"I will return soon."

He stepped down and marched away out of her view. What a superb man. When all this worked out, he might go away. She must not, could not, let him leave, or what would she do? She had no way to keep him, no right to his company. Unless she could think of a way to encourage him to stay. Fiona set her mind to this problem, warming herself in the sunshine of a fine London day.

****

Philip entered the sober offices of the Archbishop of Canterbury and dealt with a saintly clerk. He was treated with deference, signed his name, paid a fee, and accepted the document, heavy with stamps and seals. He folded it into his breast pocket and walked back out into the sun. He would tell Fiona; or he would wait. Better wait, he decided, for what happens next. If Cameron came back, he was prepared to handle him. Wait and see.

He hurried back to the carriage and hopped in. Fiona smiled, touching his heart.

"That did not take long. A host of clergy went by, all as solemn as could be. What is located here, exactly?"

"Solicitors and barristers. Church offices. Courts."

"Very impressive. There must have been twenty of them, striding along in black robes like dusky crows. Shall we go home now?"

"How would you like to have lunch? I know a place."

"I would love that," she exclaimed.

Another rap on the roof. "Aye?"

"One Two Three Albemarle Street, Jem, just off Piccadilly."

"Aye, I know it, sir."

The panel slid shut. Back out into traffic they went.

Fiona glowed with what seemed an inner light. Who could tire of that face, her shining, reddish hair, or that smile? She was resilient and full of high spirits. Philip considered himself a prudent man. He had known her four days; the whole fascination could wear off. It was not in his nature to act impulsively. His responsibilities had increased; he had a lot to do. The war dragged on, would catch him up again, and possibly kill him. He had no time for Fiona Seymour.

But he could not walk away. She needed his help, and he needed her. His yearning to have her, all of her, had become a tangible thing he now carried around. He entertained fantasies of her in his bed, her bed, any bed. Once she was there, he kissed her lush skin, whispered his heart, took her and took her until he was satisfied and so was she. He heard her laughter as he did little things to tempt and tease her.

Fiona was only nineteen years old, and he was a trifle jaded. A lifetime had been crammed into the seven years between them. There had been women, some of whom did not know his name or that he was English. He had blended in with sailors in dockside bawdyhouses and taverns on both sides of the channel, waiting for information. As long as they were clean, he had no regrets, was courteous, and paid up. He could not go back to that.

Nearly drowning had changed him. Trying to get his breath in hospital, the fatigue that had eaten into his muscles, the racking cough. No, he was a different man now. He had met Fiona, and she held out hope and affection, friendship and love. In her innocence, in her strength, she made him feel whole again.

He took her gloved hand in his, and she dazzled him when she smiled.

"Have you been long away from London, Philip?" she inquired.

"Two years. The house on Park Street was leased for a time. I reclaimed it, then got busy and was in and out of town unpredictably. I may lease it again. I have to get back to Hampshire."

"Oh," she said, her voice small.

"But not today, pretty Fiona." Philip took her in his arms and kissed her rosy mouth. Breathed her fragrance and cherished her soft womanliness. He had a cold place in his belly, the icy cold of the sea, and Fiona almost reached it. But she would, if he had his way, and then he could be warm again. And he would love and cherish her, and keep her safe.

Fiona, despite the rattle of the old carriage, felt the journey through the crowded streets to be cushioned on the clear May air. She would have liked to ride on forever beside Philip, to some wondrous place. Although anywhere he was seemed magical. These past days had been crammed with activity and events, but the greatest, the most impressive, was Philip. Without him, she would have been lost.

She backtracked from this. If it had come to it, she would have managed, and that should still be her aim. If Philip needed to go home, there was no more to say. At this idea, her courage drooped. She leaned a bit his way, seeking comfort. He was here now. If she did not think of a tactic to delay his departure, honorably, of course, she would just have to endure the loss.

The carriage halted before a tidy rose-red brick building.

"Here we are, Fiona," Philip said, as Walsh opened the door. He stepped down and raised his hand for hers. She took it and alighted. Two large pottery urns either side of a black paneled door spilled a variety of blossoms in a colorful array. A square brass sign affixed to the wall read CLARKE'S.

Philip opened the door, and she walked in. The small interior consisted mostly of a large marble-topped counter. A man in a good suit and linen shirt, his cravat precise, stood behind it. His expression softened.

"Why, Lord Colbourne, after all this time."

"It is I, Mr. Clarke. How have you fared?"

"The business is fine, Cook is mean as a scalded cat, and the food is excellent." His countenance altered. "Young Tristan, you must remember him, took ship two days ago. We think bound for Belgium. That was the rumor."

"Good lad. I will keep him in my thoughts."

The man nodded. "But forgive me, sir, and my lady. Luncheon?"

"Please."

Mr. Clarke led them along a hallway and into a dining area at the back of the building. There were scattered folk ranged about. They were led on to a table by windows, looking out on a tiny enclosed rose garden. It was a unique atmosphere.

The man snapped his fingers for a waiter, who rushed to them, then Clarke bowed and walked away.

"All this grandeur is hidden from the street," she said in wonder.

"It is a special place."

The waiter hovered.

"We would like a chilled bottle of Heidsieck. And a few of your cheese things, whatever they are called."

"Cheddar twists, my lord. Yes, sir, right away."

Philip turned to her, his gaze intimate. Fiona's heart skipped two or three beats.

"I have never been in such an elegant place," she whispered. "Is it private?"

"In a way. You have to know about it. Word gets around." He leaned an elbow on the table.

"Clarke was my father's personal secretary. When my parents died, he was willed a good amount for his years of service and bought this building. The cook, Lola, a hot-blooded Italian, may or may not be his lover. Tristan is his youngest son."

Waiters brought the wine in a silver bucket of cracked ice. One of them poured into etched crystal glasses, and the familiar bubbles rose. Fiona, out in the world with a gorgeous man, was overjoyed.

They toasted.

"To the loveliest lady in London," he quietly said.

"To the charming man who thinks so," she answered.

They drank. It was like swallowing fiery ice.

"How good. I can see I have been drinking inferior wine at balls."

They drank more. A plate was placed on the table with thin baked cheese sticks. They nibbled these.

"Delicious."

The wine made a little buzz in her breast, the cheddar twist tangy. Fiona sighed. Mercy, this was living.

Fiona studied the menu card, and Philip studied her. He refreshed her glass, noting the drink made her eyes sparkle. She was obviously enjoying herself. What little it took to make her happy.

"What appeals to you, Fiona?"

"I confess, I have no idea what is on offer. For instance, what is pasta?"

"A noodle, rolled out thinly and cooked in many shapes. The noodle type is suited to the sauce, I am told. Remember the cook is Italian." He helped out. "I think I will have the steak pizzaiola. That is a thin beefsteak in a marinara sauce, which is made of seasoned tomatoes. Tomatoes are still avoided in British cuisine, but I have eaten them in various dishes and they are tasty."

"Suggest something lighter, please."

He read the choices. "Then perhaps you would try the lemon carbonara. That is a long, thin pasta with bits of Italian bacon and an egg yolk."

"My, how do you know all this?"

He pointed to the card. "I read the Italian description."

She appeared awestruck. "You speak Italian?"

"I do. When I was sixteen, I traveled to Rome and Naples with my tutor."

"Oh, mercy. How sophisticated. Thank you; I will have the lemon dish."

He ordered, more wine was poured, and she ate another cheddar twist, her green eyes on him.

Her lovely smile.

"How much you know, Philip. What was Italy like?"

"Hot. Very ancient. Friendly people who laughed a lot, drank quantities of wine, and loved to eat. Highly emotional, Italians sort of run headlong at life. I was taken around to all the cultural sites, which were impressive, but every meal was a feast. Being a growing lad, I ate quantities of everything. I would like to go back."

"I have been nowhere," she revealed, "not even to the seaside, somewhere like Brighton. No use to suggest a vacation to my father."

He pictured her in Southampton. "You would like the sea."

"Of course, I would. Now that I have my money, I might go on a journey."

This disturbed him. "To Italy?"

"No, silly, to the sea. I am not ready for the continent."

He imagined them together in Italy. "I would take you," he announced. Then regretted it.

"Oh? How far is it to Brighton?" she wondered.

She had misunderstood, and he was saved. "Some fifty miles south, depending on the roads. Overnight at Guildford, perhaps, then arrive the next day."

"Mmmm. Sounds exciting."

"Shall we go?" he asked, dreaming she would say yes.

But waiters appeared with the food. Fiona watched everything as they placed the plates and offered shreds of a soft cheese. More wine, serviettes, and they began. But she faltered.

"I do not know how to eat these noodles," she whispered.

"Wind strands around the fork, using the spoon."

He demonstrated the technique, and Fiona wound some of the noodle, then poked it into her mouth. She chewed and blinked.

"Hugely flavorful! Mmmm, lemon and cheese. A different sort of salty bacon. I love it! How is yours?"

He swallowed. "Perfection."

Fiona scooted the noodles around the plate, got strands to stick together, then ate them with gusto. "So many tastes! Just yummy."

Philip's heart seemed to enlarge, as he enjoyed her zest for the meal. It could be a life's work giving her pleasure. He ate his beef and considered doing just that.

Chapter Eight

Fiona was having a sensationally good time. She simmered with enjoyment as she ate the exotic food and drank the wine, feeling very worldly. She scooped up the last of the dish, completely sated. "A fabulous luncheon, Philip. Thank you for bringing me here. I will remember it always."

"As will I," he remarked. He filled their glasses, draining the bottle. "Shall we be a small part Italian, you and I, pretty Fiona? 'Mangia bene, ridi spesso, ama molto'?"

The words were musical in his deep voice. "What did you say?"

"A common phrase. 'Eat well, laugh often, love much.' "

"Yes! I would like to live as they do. Right here in England, pasta in every shape." She had a good drink. "And lots of fine wines."

"Consider dessert?"

"I cannot," she said with regret.

"Nor I." He raised his arm, and the waiter hastened to the table with a paper. Philip read, took out his pocketbook, and laid down a bill. "Tell Cook that our meal was superb."

"Yes, sir, I will, thank you."

The waiter held her chair, and Fiona gathered her reticule and gloves. Philip took her arm, and they left

Clarke's. The carriage waited at a short distance. Jem saw them and urged the horses their way. Walsh, ever on the job, jumped down to hold the door.

"Tell Jem we would go home, if you please, Walsh."

"Yes, Miss Fiona."

She and Philip got in, and the vehicle rolled away. He leaned very close, his dark eyes luminous. He kissed her somewhat fiercely and poked his tongue right in her mouth! Fiona nudged his tongue with hers, rather cross at the invasion, but that encouraged him. She was astounded, then sensations of delight crept over her.

Philip gathered her to him, broke the kiss, held her tighter, and breathed into her ear. Gooseflesh covered her entire left arm and leg. With all that noodle in her tummy, her stays pinched, and she could scarcely breathe. This intensified everything, and she began to worry she would faint and make a fool of herself.

"Fiona," he whispered, "I adore every particle of you."

"Well—"

"Even if I cannot see all of your charms, at least not yet. But I soon will."

His hand moved ominously toward her breast. She clutched her reticule, and gasped, "In a carriage?"

He laughed. "No, not in a carriage. The trip is too short."

Now she felt ridiculous. "You are fooling."

"Fiona, I would give everything I have to make you mine."

"Oh, really? Hand it over. This was said to me once before, but I knew the fellow would not part with a shilling."

"It is a metaphorical statement," he objected, "indicating a raging desire you are too naïve to understand."

"Is that your opinion?" she huffed. "Men tend to think only they know about, er, desire, as you call it."

"What do *you* call it?" he asked.

Fiona sidestepped. "I have no such terms."

"Ah, me. I will just have to teach you some."

She had no reply. Just looked at him.

"And I will love doing it," he added. "Darling girl," he murmured, stroking her cheek with his fingers.

"You are flirting," she accused.

"At last you understand."

Her temper sparked. "Worse, you are toying with me. With my emotions. Because you know I have little experience. I am just an ignorant person you get satisfaction in teasing."

He denied this. "Do I seem so cruel? No, Fiona, I am sincere in what I have said."

She hardly knew what to think. It all cluttered her head. "I do not know quite what you mean, Philip," she admitted.

"I mean I find you fresh, honest, and beautiful in all your ways. I like to hold and kiss you. I like talking with you. I would intensely like to take you to my bed. Or yours, if you prefer."

Her jaw dropped, and she quickly shut it. "Well, do people—uh, what am I supposed to say? The fact that you—that I let you kiss me and I like it? You think I am—that I would? Do that?"

"I am heavily attracted to you, Fiona. That is no sin. And I am not easy to please, I would have you know. I find you to be a fantastic woman, and it is my nature to say so. Do not get the wind up. You have put me in a spin for the last four days and nights."

Her heart tensed. "So, our relations must change?"

"Inevitably."

Tears sprang to her eyes. "I must give you all you *desire*, or you will go away?" She turned aside. "Stop. This is all a farce to you."

He turned her back to him. "Marry me, Fiona."

Fiona was enraged. What gall! She would hate him for years.

Dammit, he had tipped his hand. Philip had meant to work his way up to such a request, but Fiona addled his mind. Now she thought him devious.

They arrived at Two Twenty. The groom opened the door and gave him a cold glance. God blast it, they had been overheard. He stepped out, elbowed the groom aside, and took her hand. Even through the glove, he felt her wrath.

She pulled her hand free. "Thank you, Jem, Walsh. That is all for now."

"Yes, miss."

The girl marched up the walk.

He reached her in two strides. "Listen, Fiona."

"Have I not listened?" she said mildly. "I have listened to everyone, all this time." She dropped the knocker. "They will find I have a lot to say, and they can listen to me for once."

The butler swung the door open, his manner amiable.

She greeted the man. "Hi ho, Sumpter. Has anything occurred?"

"Aye, Miss Fiona." He lifted a brown envelope. "This was delivered by messenger."

She took it. "Thank you. I will be in the drawing room."

Philip followed after her. Damnation, would she turn him down without a hearing? They sat on the sofa. "Fiona, dear," he began.

"Oh, just turn it off, Philip." She tore open the envelope. It appeared to be a long legal document. She read down the page. "Well, this does beat all. I am to be sued if I do not respond to that summons, the one I got before. By Willis Skeinfold, Earl of Cameron, for 'breach of promise, and the return of funds legitimately paid to satisfy a marriage contract.' "

Philip read over it. "Ha. Your father skinned him and got the five thousand in advance. Either Cameron is the stupidest fellow that ever lived, or your old man was the smartest."

"Can he do this? I have the contract, not him."

"You are dealing with an obsessed man, and he has snagged a lawyer who will agree with him. He has tried about everything. I believe he will never give up, Fiona." Ah, Philip realized, this could all go his way. "I fear that the only way to cut Cameron loose and quell the whole matter is to take drastic action."

"What action?"

"First, you made no promise to him of any kind; your deceased father did. Second, we must convince him you are already married."

"Perfect nonsense!" she cried and made to throw the papers into the fire. He caught her hand.

"No, we must keep those for the present. He has built a case, and so must we. When are you to appear at the solicitor's offices?"

"Tomorrow at two of the clock."

"We will be there." Philip rapidly plotted. A plan formed, if she would trust him and agree. "In the carriage, Fiona, I spoke in some haste."

"Humph."

"While you waited for me at Doctor's Commons—that is, I have been thinking, seriously thinking, and I know…um, the thing is"—he took the paper from his pocket—"I acquired this." He showed it to her.

She looked over the fancy scrollwork, the stamps and seals. "What is it?"

"A special license, to allow a couple to marry when and where they like."

"Great! You will use it to convince Cameron?"

Philip felt he was digging a very deep hole. "My object was to convince you."

Fiona leaned back on the sofa and laughed gaily. "The whole city has gone crazy; folks will run mad through the streets. Some horrid vapor has blown over us all, a subtle poison. Are you serious, Philip? Only a simpleton would fall for such a hoax. Which, I grant, Cameron may well be."

"Not if it is true."

She frowned, her straight brows dipping toward her freckled nose.

"I meant what I said!" He took a deep breath. "Would you marry me, Fiona?"

Her eyes widened. "What? A wandering sailor who may or not be an earl?"

Guilt struck him. "About that, I need to say further—"

She leaned away. "I *thought* that was a fantasy. An earl, indeed! You are impossible. We do not have a single common acquaintance who can vouch for you.

And you only know scraps about me, so it is quite bonkers to even suggest such a ruse. Do you not realize, if such a marriage was actual, it would be a lifetime commitment? And you would go off to war again? I never heard of such an irrational idea."

"I adore you, Fiona."

"So you said. How long do you suppose that will last? I am nothing extra," she said mournfully. Her lower lip trembled. "I have been nowhere and have seen no balloons go up, unlike ladies you mentioned. So the whole thing is loony! I am caught in a web others have woven. Sued by a toad! Ruined and disgraced when I have done nothing wrong." Her green eyes became accusing. "God save me, you want the money I put in the bank just today!"

"Certainly I do not. Forget the money, your father and Cameron, the ton, the gossip sheets, and the whole confusion. This is just you and me, Fiona. Yes, I am who I have said I am, and I have recently added another title to my burdens."

"I do not care to hear about your honors and titles. I will go tomorrow to this solicitor or whatever he is and face him down. I will not give Cameron tuppence, and what can they do? Throw me into prison?"

"Not if I am there, as your husband."

Fiona stood and pulled the nearby bell cord. She sat down again, her expression a blend of dismay and determination. A tap, and the maid peeped in the door.

"Yes, miss?"

"Tea, please, Daisy."

"Right away." The door closed.

"Besides," he continued, "I would not like you to be alone. Cameron might try something rash."

"Such as?"

"Kidnapping you to force a union."

"Fie. He would not dare."

Philip had to work his way back into her affections. And he better get busy, or she might have Sumpter escort him out the door. The poor fellow would try.

****

Tea renewed Fiona's courage. She would face this false suitor and his legal charlatan and speak her mind. Just let anyone try to force her into anything. She would bite and claw. All the insults and affronts her father had piled on her for years had solidified into rock, and she would not be moved.

She sipped the tea, her glance sliding to Philip. Too bad she would never sleep in his bed. As he had suggested. The thought and accompanying image gave her a shiver. Bizarre man. To play tricks on her one after another was too mean of him. Four days! Did she really *know* who he was? Had he told the truth about anything?

How could she get even? A way would present itself. She smoothed her skirt. "So, Philip. You got this license."

He appeared weary. "I did. A moment of hubris, I confess. A tide of longing, a stiff current, and I went under an emotional wave, thinking you might care for me. I see now I was in error."

This was mystifying. Would he take back all those things he had said?

"No harm done." He sighed. "The license was only a small expense."

"What?" she asked, surprised. "You had to pay?"

"Twenty guineas, plus five pounds stamp duty."

She was amazed. What an amorous thing to do! "Without asking me first?"

"It was a gamble, Fiona. By a hungry man."

"Well, but…you thought that I cared for you enough to, right out of the blue—"

Back he came to enfold her in his embrace. "When you are in my arms, Fiona, I am certain of your affections. You kiss me with your whole self. Almost. I want the rest."

"Oh."

"Absolutely."

A small silence fell. He meant none of this! The awful man would pay for his ribbing. She decided to fix him. "All right," she said, seeming to agree. "I will marry you, Philip. Before or after the solicitor?"

He looked directly at her, his manner circumspect. "Before."

A hot flush passed over her skin, her cheeks burned, her scalp tingled. She opened her mouth to tell him she was joking, but he kissed her lips, his arms strong, the scent of him maddening. Fiona's words dissolved and ran away.

They cuddled on the sofa, and Philip soaked up Fiona's nearness. However, he was not deceived by her agreement. The girl meant to be taking her revenge for his insolence, but when they kissed, she forgot. She was as eager as he for loving intimacy. That fool Cameron would herd her right into Philip's bed.

He had been out all day and may have had a missive from Malrose. Why was Cameron still free to make trouble? And why was the man so persistent? It had to be the money. Secure Fiona and it would be all his.

Philip would never agree. Fiona belonged to him, and he would not let her go. Malrose was perhaps having the traitor watched until others were revealed. Cameron was not slick enough to transport and deliver funds to the French; it must be someone higher up. He puzzled over this. Who?

The maid came to collect the tea tray, jangling his nerves. To soothe his mind, he began to make love to Fiona. He inhaled the flowery aroma of her reddish hair, a silken mass. Caressed the curve of her throat and she turned to him, her green eyes mellow. His heart flipped over. He cupped her pert chin and kissed her soft lips.

Philip brushed his fingers over her shoulder, and his hand gently descended to her elbow. He put her arm around his neck to hold her closer and cradled her breast in his palm. She groaned, arched toward him, and he was hers for eternity.

To his amazement, she was swiftly all over him. Her hand went into his hair. Next, she slipped it inside his coat, examined the buttons on his shirt, swooped down to the waist of his breeches, and he got a grip on her.

Or thought he did. If she sat any closer, she would be on his other side. She bit his ear; he lost the power of speech and could only make a garbled noise. When she licked his neck and undid his cravat, he had to call a halt.

"Fiona," he breathed.

"What a delicious man you are, Philip. I trust this display of passion is because now we are betrothed?"

"That does not give you the right to go overboard on a sofa. Time and place. But what a sugarplum you are. When is dinner?"

"Well," she protested, "you only just had tea."

"I have to leave you for an hour or two."

She gave him a shove. "I should get used to this! You eat, drink, and then depart."

"I must go home and check my messages. Remember Malrose. I am still on duty."

She tilted her head. "La, la."

"King and country, girl. But I will be back and, after dinner, explain to you about that balloon going up. My love," he murmured, leaning closer. "You smell of roses."

"That is my bath soap. Well, go then, you wandering sailor. Dinner at seven?"

"That gives me time. Dear Fiona, I value your good humor."

"Humph. It is a disguise to save my pride when I do not get my way. This is often the case."

He kissed her cheek. "Delightful woman. See me out."

They strolled to the foyer, arm in arm. Sumpter came along and hastened to open the door.

"Thank you, Sumpter. Back at seven, Fiona."

"I will be here. Stay safe."

****

Philip went down the sidewalk, his mind on Malrose and the spies. And on Fiona. Jesus, she had instantly turned wild. Those small hands moving over him had put him into a frenzy. If he got her in bed, he would have to guard himself from injury. He crossed Green and headed down Park Street, laughing to himself. His sweet virgin was a cyclone, but by God, he was ready to contain her.

173

Nearly home, he had the creeping impression he was being followed. Stopped abruptly and pretended to adjust his boot. Bent down and saw a dark shape cut behind a clump of rhododendron. Philip straightened, went on up his walk, and stepped to the front door. Quietly swung off the porch, slipped behind the bushes to the corner of the house, and well hidden by shrubbery, regained the sidewalk. The fellow, a small man, skulked along, headed away from the house. Phillip grabbed him and put an arm tightly around his neck.

"Who the fuck are you?" he demanded.

"Nobody, mate, nobody!" he squealed. "Doin' a job, thas all. Swear it, meanin' you no harm, sir."

Philip gave him a shake, and the man lost his balance. He hauled him upright. "Who paid you to follow me?"

"Toff I met, over to the park. Yesterday, it was. Give me sixpence to watch the house over there at Two Twenty Green. Tell him who comes and goes. Said it was about a lady, so's I thought I would make a jot of cash. Meant no harm, sir, I swear it."

"When will you see him again?"

"Now. I was just goin' back there. Seen you go in Two Twenty and visit, then when you come out—but I never knowed you seen me."

"Where are you meeting this fellow?"

"The upper Brook Street gate."

Philip reached into his pocket and withdrew a shilling. "My friend, the man who engaged you is a dangerous killer. Take this and run the other way."

"Cor blimey!" he cried, gazing at the valuable coin. "Yes sir, yes sir, I be gone."

The fellow vanished into the darkness. Philip retraced his steps to the corner of Brook and headed up it to Park Lane, paused under a leafy sycamore, but saw no one loitering about. He crossed the street when the way was clear and walked on. When he thought it prudent, he circled back through the park and stopped, keeping the Brook Street gate in view. The light was poor, but Philip saw a man step out of the deep shadows and glance about. He leaned on the gate and lit a cigar. Philip caught a whiff of cheap tobacco.

He waited. The man smoked restlessly and paced about impatiently as the minutes passed. Then he abruptly tossed away the stub of his cigar and walked rapidly away toward Marble Arch. At a discreet distance, Philip followed.

At the Arch, he got into a waiting hackney. Philip signaled to another and called to the jarvey, "Follow that cab just pulling out. The third one."

"Eh?"

"Do it. Do not lose him, and a shilling is yours."

"Yes, sir, get in."

Off the first cab went, his jarvey quickly catching up. They followed along Oxford Street, the traffic busy. Philip craned out the window to keep his prey in view. The first cab went around the Circus, then turned onto Regent Street. After a few blocks, it halted at Maddox Street, and the fellow got out. Philip signaled, and his cab halted a half block back. He stepped down.

"Excellent." He flipped the jarvey the coin and walked after the man, but he did not go far. At the second house on Maddox, he fitted a key and walked inside, slamming the door. Philip had never seen him before and considered what to do. He walked back toward Regent and to an alley behind the row of houses.

He stepped down it, startling several feral cats, which snarled and howled, then raced away. The alley was muddy and littered with trash. There was no gate behind the second house, but Philip easily cleared the low fence. The area dark as pitch, he picked his way through numerous obstacles up to the house. At the corner, a room was lit, and four men were seated at a table. He got as close as he dared. They appeared to be discussing papers spread out before them.

One was the man he had followed, who seemed to be reporting to the others. One was the bastard Harley. The third, dressed in evening clothes, dark hair, goatee, looked to be in charge. And the last was the weasel Cameron. Philip could not hear a word, but he had found the meeting place, a valuable tidbit to relay to Malrose.

After an interval studying them, he turned to leave and knocked against a broken barrel. Over it went with a crash, shouts erupted from the house, and the window was thrown up. Philip lunged headlong for the fence, making a huge racket, and leapt over it as shots rang out. He heard the whiz of a ball as another tore through his coat sleeve.

He dropped to his hands and knees and crawled quickly along, gained his feet at Regent Street, and ran as fast as he could toward the Circus. There, he lost himself in the crowds. Breathing hard, he kept on toward the Arch, crossed Oxford Street, and hailed a hackney.

"Park Street at Culross," he called.

"Aye."

Philip got in and sat back as they rolled away. Jesus, he was filthy and stank of cat shit. He felt his torn coat sleeve, and his fingers came away bloody. He shook his head at his own foolhardy actions and grinned. They did not get him, and he had some confidence they never would.

****

Fiona watched Philip leave, and the butler closed the door.

"Will you please tell Cook we will be two for dinner?" she asked.

"I will, miss. At seven."

"Thank you, Sumpter."

She drifted up the stairs thinking over the wonderful day. The amusing talk, the being together for hours on end. A fortune in the bank was in her name alone. Just let somebody try to take it back! In her chamber, she fell into her chair, remembering the fine restaurant and the very best champagne. People she knew would never believe it, nor credit someone like Philip Laughton to be in her acquaintance.

He was enchanting. Everything a man should be. Tall and strong and sweet. He said extravagant things and kissed her at every opportunity, so it was difficult—no—impossible, to resist him.

Fiona felt a terrible stab of remorse. She should not have said she would marry him, just to give him a pinch. It was mean. Now she would have to squirm out of it. Apologize, even. Likely, he had not believed it. Philip was very intelligent and surely saw through her deception. She propped her feet on the footstool.

So touching that he had gotten a costly special license, hopeful that she would agree. Or whatever he meant by it. It had become a little hazy in her mind. Maybe it was just to fool Cameron after all, and Philip was teasing her with it. *A gamble by a hungry man*, he had said. She was proud to have his regard. It gave Fiona a sense of her own worth, which she had sadly lacked.

No man she had met or imagined could even come close to Philip, her handsome sailor and special friend. If only she could have his escort to a grand ball. She would wear her very best and show him off as they danced and danced. The other girls would turn blue at the sight of him.

At the very edges of this daydream, Fiona scarcely believed a word he had said. It was simply fantastic, the shipwreck, Oxford, an earldom, the man Malrose, and not a whit of evidence to back it all up.

Malrose, whoever he was, knew him, as did the man at Clarke's. Random folks called him my lord. But Philip had not told her from the first that he had a title. Gentlemen were generally not slow to boast about their rank. Philip had not spoken until he was cornered. Strange, all very strange. *The ninth Earl of Colbourne*, he had declared. Nine of them? Impossible.

Fiona sorted over these facts and the lack of them and dozed in the sunshine. Drowsy, she recalled his kisses and the way he had made her feel, completely carefree. The rascal had touched her breast. Deliberately, with his whole hand. It had felt tremendous. She had then become rather excited, not to say carried away. Without her conscious volition, she nearly climbed over him. It was terribly foolish, but Philip did not seem to mind. His hair had felt luscious, thick and soft. He had tasted nice, too, male and kind of salty. Like the sea.

Lawsy, her entire life had tipped over like a basket of apples and she was rolling every which way. All in a very short time, she had become somebody else, or perhaps, emerged as the true Fiona. It was unbelievable either way.

Fiona could not think what would happen at the so-called solicitor's office, with the viper Cameron, with Philip and his spies, or any of it. But she was bound and determined to take the ride, wherever it led.

And of course, now that she had money, that fairytale cottage in Surrey was waiting.

****

Philip arrived home.

Reston held his nose. "My dod," he croaked. "Wha has happen?"

"Got bogged down in an alley. Have my bath prepared, please."

He trotted up the stairs, his arm burning. Damn them, they had winged him.

Pearce waited. "My lord." He looked dubious. "Difficulties?"

"Some." He quickly stripped off his ruined coat and shirt and examined the damage. The ball had been deflected somewhat by his clothing or the range. A strip of flesh on his upper arm had been grazed and still oozed blood. It had been a near thing.

"Oh, sir!" Pearce cried.

"Not too bad," Philip reckoned. Two footmen arrived with his bath paraphernalia, and he turned away. No use roiling the household.

"I will bring aid," Pearce intoned and hurried away. Philip retreated to his dressing room and mopped at the cut with his shirt. He pushed off his boots and, holding the ragged shirt in place, shed his breeches and smalls.

Pearce returned. "I brought the salve and bandages. The arm should be cleaned."

"I will clean all of me. I smell like a sewer." He stepped into the tub, sat down, and plunged the arm into the hot water. "Christ crucified!" he shouted. The water stung like a hoard of wasps. Pearce ladled soapy suds over it.

Gradually, it all got done, even his hair. Philip hated cats. Hated goddamned Cameron and all the trouble the fool had brought him. He climbed out of the water. Pearce briskly dried him off, as Philip pressed cotton waste to the injury. The healing salve concoction was applied, and the valet wrapped a bandage around his arm, his face troubled.

"I believe that will hold, my lord. But take care."

"I shall. It hurts like the devil. I am out for dinner."

Clothes were provided, and Philip got into them.

Pearce fussed. "My lord, I realize you are on duty, but may I point out you need rest?"

"No time for that. Did I receive any messages today?"

"No, sir, not to my knowledge."

Where was Malrose? Philip had the notion he was somehow holding the bag. What the hell was going on?

He sat down and wrote the man a note.

Tonight I encountered a man who had been watching Two Twenty Green, Fiona Seymour's home. Caught the watcher and located his contact waiting on Park Lane. Unseen, I trailed him to number Three Maddox Street and via a window, found him with three other men. One was Harley, one was Cameron, and another well-dressed, authoritative fellow, black hair, medium build, short goatee, seemed in charge. When discovered, they took a couple of shots at me, but I got away. For God's sake, keep in touch. I am out on a string here.

C.

He sealed the note, addressed it, thanked Pearce, and returned downstairs, Reston looking him over and sniffing.

"Much improved, my lord."

"Thank you, Reston. There were no messages today?"

"No, sir."

"Very good. I want this note delivered first thing tomorrow. Back later."

Philip walked out of the house. Blast Malrose. Was he supposed to win the war all on his own? He proceeded to Two Twenty, watchful all the while, his sore arm a reminder of just what sort of villains he was dealing with.

****

Fiona, in a fine gown of pink sprigged muslin, the neckline trimmed with lace, waited in the drawing room for Philip to arrive. When he came, she would immediately tell him she had not been serious regarding the marriage. She would say she had thought about it, and—it must be something to save face and not make Philip cross. Best confess she was giving him a tweak, but that sounded cold. One did not jest when offered marriage. Or a semblance thereof.

It was darling of him to be of help to her. He had no reason to. She was nobody special, not family, not anything. Curses. Was she still listening to her father's insults? She *was* worthy and may become someone remarkable, if given a chance to develop. She would gain some talents, learn, and improve.

The ton may be waiting to put her on the shelf, but she was young and strong. Nineteen was not past it, not old. The whole snooty lot of them conspired to beat her and other girls down. She had outlasted her father, and the ton seemed another set of chains she must cast off. In fact, she had already done so. Just to think the thought was radical, but so were the last few days, unchaperoned, amply kissed and hugged, and taken about town to hidden restaurants.

How could she ever give Philip up? Not that she had any choice in the matter. He would leave, as soon as he had eaten enough. Go back to the navy and his duties. The thought of his glorious self being damaged was ghastly, and she would never know! Perhaps he would write to her occasionally. No, he would not, she sighed, and fought back tears. She must stop thinking all these things.

She heard voices. Philip had come! Her pulse fluttered, her palms went damp. She would lose her mind and collapse.

Sumpter announced him. "Mr. Laughton, miss."

Philip sauntered in. "Hello. Am I early or late?"

Fiona controlled herself and smiled. "Neither. Do sit down."

He sat beside her on the sofa, and smelled good, like incense. They gazed at each other.

"Philip," she began. "About tomorrow."

He took her hand. "Now, Fiona, do not worry. I will handle the solicitor or whatever the vagrant is, and

Cameron, too. Never think I do not have a plan."

The man *always* had a plan! "No, it is just that, well—"

"I assure you it will all be taken care of. Dear girl, you seem pressed. Nothing bad is going to happen."

She had to speak the truth and, to get his attention, took his arm.

He pulled away, his expression pained. "Damn," he whispered and held it away from her.

"What is the matter?" she asked. "Have you—did you hurt yourself?"

He bit his lips. "Just a scratch."

His face told her otherwise. "Let me see."

"No, it is nothing."

"I do not believe you! Show me."

He drew a breath.

"Show me," she insisted.

He stood and took off his coat. Fiona's heart twitched. His neckcloth and shirt went, and she nearly swooned to see him in all his magnificence. Tanned skin, dark hair on his broad chest. An inadequate bandage wrapped around his left upper arm was stained with blood.

She leapt from her seat. "God in heaven, what happened?"

"I uh, followed a lead on some of our spies, peered in a back window, was seen, and had to run for it. They took a couple of shots at me, but I escaped. My man fixed it up."

She raced to the doors, and cried, "Sumpter!" The butler was right there. "Mr. Laughton has been hurt. Could you bring some of Cook's medication cream? And some bandaging?"

"Yes, miss."

She hurried back to him. He was slumped on the sofa, holding his bandage.

"Do not worry. Cook has a mixture that will heal anything and take away the pain. Do you have pain?" she anxiously inquired.

"Not unless I bump into it."

"Oh, oh," she grieved.

Sumpter returned with a tray, the jar of mixture, cotton waste, and a roll of bandaging. "Shall I attend him, Miss Fiona?"

"No, I will. Thank you, Sumpter."

Fiona had no idea what she was doing but had to help Philip. She cautiously undid the small knot and unwrapped the bandage. Blood had soaked through it, and it was sticky.

"My valet dressed it. Not so good, eh?"

He had a valet? "You walked here and disturbed it. You should rest that arm." The injury was two or three inches long, and she dabbed at it with the cotton until it looked clean. Then, with one finger, she carefully put on a good deal of the mixture.

"Now, wait a minute or two, and it will feel better." Fiona wanted to kiss and comfort him but paused to let the medicine do its work.

Gradually, his expression eased. "That feels much better. It is cooling and numbing."

"Oh, good. I have used it for cuts and so on all my life. It is very effective. Just sit back and relax until it does not bleed anymore."

He did so. Fiona filled her eyes; mercy, he was glorious. What more could she do for him? What could she say?

"You must not take such chances, Philip."

"I got valuable information. I located the meeting house and have seen the leader of the spies."

"Did you know him?"

"No, but Cameron and Harley were there. If I chance to see the man again, I will recognize him. I informed Malrose."

"Then let *him* be shot at!" This was horrible! "Oh, Philip. What if they had killed you?"

"Then my worries would be over," he wryly remarked.

She wanted to smack him. "What about mine?"

His devilish smile. "Ah, sweetheart. You would care?"

"Of course I would. See, the bleeding has stopped."

He glanced at it. "So it has. What is in this stuff?" he asked.

"Cook will not say. I know witch hazel is involved, goose fat, and some herbs. I think maybe it can be bandaged again. Thicker, so it will be protected and you can stand to touch it."

"Will you do this?"

"Yes." She took up the bandaging and fashioned a pad. Tore the cloth, then gently put it over the wound, wrapped the roll around his upper arm, very muscled, she noted. Circled around and around, then tore it again to form two ends, which she knotted.

"Wonderful. It feels fine now."

"I suspect that was a fib, but I hope so. Be easy with it, Philip."

She helped him put his shirt back on and, gazing into his dark eyes, buttoned it. He fashioned his neckcloth ably and tucked in his shirt. Fiona put a cushion under his elbow.

"You are not cold without your coat?"

"Not with you next to me."

Now she felt like smiling again. "You are incorrigible, Philip."

"So I am told. May I have a kiss?"

"You may."

She leaned over him and kissed his mouth, then his cheek, then his ear. "Do not hurt yourself again. You have sacrificed enough."

"How much is enough?" he asked. "The war rages on. These traitorous men want it to end, not for righteous victory, but for profit. They do not care about Napoleon and his fever dreams of ruling the world."

Fiona was up to the chin with concern for him.

"England faces invasion, Fiona. Every day our forces are working to stop it. To save the country from destruction. I cannot fall back from that. I have to do all I can."

Tears welled up. Philip was so honorable and brave. "I do not want to lose you," she whispered.

"Dear girl. I do adore you."

She could not ask him to cease his efforts. He was bound to act for England. How noble.

"If you go away, Philip, I will wait. To hear from you, that is. That you are all right."

He studied her face. "You would wait for me?"

"Yes, if you wish it. If it would not be a burden."

"You angel," he said, and they kissed.

A tap at the door, and Sumpter stepped in. "Dinner is served, Miss Fiona."

"Thank you, Sumpter. Do you want your coat, Philip?"

"Yes, please."

Fiona helped him into it, and they strolled to the dining room, hand in hand. Philip Laughton was her hero in every instance. She finally acknowledged to herself that she loved him, loved him entirely, over everything else. Absolutely everything. Now what?

Chapter Nine

Philip ate heartily, the meal being first-rate. He was certain Fiona cared for him, loved her concerned manner over his injury, and her gentle attention. She would wait for him if he went away. It quite set him up to think so. He enjoyed the quality wine and hardly knew why he had gotten that special license. Before this, he had shown little interest in getting married but had gone there as if unable to help himself.

He just had to, hoping against all reasonable odds the girl might agree to have him. So he could have her. It was as if he had been in a trance. Philip chewed. He had left her waiting in the carriage, unattended! Madness all around. The fact was, he had fallen for Fiona Seymour like a schoolboy. He ate more beets. Which way should he go? Hie to the church, or call the insanity off and head for Hampshire?

She raised her wine glass to her lips, and his heart stopped. Gazed soulfully at him and it started up again with a jolt. He could *not* let her go. The spirits were guiding him; this was meant to be. The Fates had not let him drown so he could find Fiona, complete himself, and make his life meaningful. She would help him to bear his obligations, the title, all of it. Soothe and comfort him, as she had with his wound. Which felt pretty good, considering.

In recompense for her caring, he would cover the

girl in jewels and anything else she wanted. Entirely love her and say so daily, so she would never leave. So she would keep on looking at him with those green eyes full of affection.

"Delicious food, Fiona. My respect for your cook grows. And for her medication."

"Your arm is better?"

"It is. It was not deep, as well as I could see."

"I did not think so. You must tell me all about it later."

Servants being in attendance, he said no more. Dishes were cleared by Daisy, and Gregg presented a plum tart. Philip ate about half of that while Fiona pecked delicately at a slice. What a love she was. He would never tire of her dear face. Full of food, he now yearned even more keenly for her delectable charms.

"Coffee in the drawing room, Gregg, if you please."

"Yes, miss."

Gregg held her chair, and Philip joined her. They returned to the drawing room and sat side by side on the sofa.

"Now, tell me," she asked.

He regaled her with the story, even about the cats.

"How scary! But to follow a man into a desperate situation, Philip. Was that wise?"

"I did not know it was desperate until I got there. Never mind all that." He was about to kiss her, but Daisy arrived with the coffee tray, and he must wait. Now Fiona had to pour and all that. Philip took the cup. They sipped, his eyes on her. She was…

"What time shall we go, Philip?"

He snapped to attention. "Where?"

"To the church. In the morning."

He went hot, cold, then hot again, right to his boots.

"Ohhhh." She sighed. "You have changed your mind."

"No, no," he gasped.

"I cannot blame you; it was a crazed idea. Let us face it, Philip. Our main objective is to defeat Cameron."

He scrambled to draw her back. "Well, how are we to do it? That contract is airtight. He can drag you around forever if you cannot show you are married."

"Is not that man Malrose after him for foul doings?" she inquired. "Cameron does not have the time to pursue me like a hound after a fox."

A defect in his scheme—must evade. "Your hair is rather foxy," he joked. "How long is it?"

She stared blankly at him.

"I would pursue you around the world, Fiona. Cameron might go as far as the Thames. However, we can work it all out."

Her face was so trusting, it gave him a guilty twinge. He must convince her he was the only man for her. Philip was prepared to do so, any way he could. Take it all the way. Marry her? Definitely! Tomorrow, she would belong to him.

Fiona was alarmed. Astounding! He was going to go through with it. If she made a commotion, he would abandon the plan and her with it. What can he be thinking? But she had seen the license, which had seemed highly official.

"Do you *want* to be married, Philip?" she asked, bewildered.

He gazed curiously at her.

"I mean…well, you know. To me."

"God," he breathed, "it sounds like paradise."

This was not how it was supposed to go. "But without a plan and all the trappings? A house and furniture?"

"People get around to that. But you have a house and I have a house, for starters."

"I would cheerfully burn this house to the foundations," she declared.

"I believe that would offend your neighbors. You can live with me."

Fiona was forced to abandon this tactic and took another. "We hardly know each other. Aside from your ability to consume large quantities of food, I do not know your habits."

"I bathe regularly, if able," he piously stated, "clean my teeth with care, since they have to last, and enjoy fresh linen daily."

She fell into helpless giggles.

He shifted closer. "I assume you do about the same, my dear. We should rub along nicely. I promise to be faithful and never grow a beard."

She clapped her hands. "That settles it, I am yours. But seriously, Philip."

"I am totally serious, Fiona."

He put his arms around her, and she was glad. When he was near, nothing made her uneasy. She helplessly loved him, after all, but did he love her? Even a little? Or was he just purely demented?

Philip had to keep it all going. "I thought to go in the morning and get the ceremony taken care of. Then, after a spot of lunch, keep the appointment at two of the clock."

"Typical you would plan for lunch," Fiona murmured. "Which ceremony?"

"The marriage."

At the word, her cheeks colored. "It will not be a sham?" she whispered.

Philip ignored this and went on. "If the appointment seems legitimate, that is. I will make sure. I am curious to see if the unknown man will be there."

She did not listen, but anxiously asked, "It is to be legal? Binding?"

He must tread cautiously. "If you want me, Fiona, as I want you. Otherwise, we have no argument to refute his claim."

Her gaze darted around the room. "Why cannot they all be arrested by officials?"

Jesus, she was panicking. He kept her in his arms. "I want very much to marry you, Fiona. More than I can say."

"Try," she suggested.

"You are perfection and have made a place in my heart."

"I trust it is not crowded with other ladies. Have you a past?"

"Everyone living has a past. Since we met, I think of you constantly." He must say more. "A great yearning overtook me to make you my own and that persists. I wildly desire you, all of you. No other woman has ever enchanted me as you do. And you care for me, I know it, I feel it. And I think you want me around to make endless love to you."

He held her face in his hands, her green eyes misty. "I have plans to do so, Fiona, and a hundred things I want to do and say. Finally, I am not about to let you go. The thought of some other man claiming your sweetness is painful. I want you to belong to me, and how else but to marry you? We are decent people. I do *not* want some back street affair. I want you as my wife, so I can ravish you frequently, make you laugh, and show you how happy we can be."

"I was not trained to be a countess," she said doubtfully.

Oh, hell, he still had not told her. "About that," Philip began, then changed course. "You are everything aristocratic. Feminine and virginal and truly special. Worthy of a prince, but take me, Fiona. Take a chance, leap into the unknown, and I will be with you."

Unexpectedly, a single tear slipped down her satin cheek, and his heart knocked as she brushed it away.

"You are sure, Philip? That this, that we—is this a wartime thing? Rash and impulsive?"

He hugged her and kissed her soft lips. Caressed her small body, a temptation of pillowed curves. "No," he murmured in her ear, "I know this is true and will be lasting. When I am with you, I am hopeful again. I have not been, Fiona, not for some time. The awful loss of my crew. The ship going down, the near-death ordeal of it. I saw my life running out like sand in an hourglass. After the hospital, I felt empty. Then I came up to London and met you, flat on your pretty face, and my life seemed to knit together again, like a broken bone."

Now, Philip triumphed, he had her. Her expression was angelic. The motherless darling had not had an ounce of approval or affection from her father. She did not know how wonderful she was.

"Really? I helped you, Philip?"

"Immensely. And you want me, too. Say it. Say you do and make it real."

"Yes, yes, I do, but this is all so fast. I mean, no banns will be read. Is that not when people take account? What the three weeks are for?"

"We do not need that, Fiona. Decide. Here and now. Marry me."

In his arm, she trembled. How young she was, how untried. Philip's emotions increased. He would do everything in his power to keep her with him, in his care, sheltered in his love. He tried to convey this silently, his whole attention on her. Kissed and held her, stroked her hair, nibbled her earlobe, and she shivered. Ran his hand over her hip, down her thigh to her knee. She did not resist. Jesus, he would be her love slave. The image of her submission to him, of her heart and soul offered up, drugged his senses.

She wavered. "You would not deceive me, would you, Philip?"

"Never, I swear it, and I will always be trustworthy. I give you my word, on my honor as a gentleman. Can you believe this?"

She rested against him, and he knew she would be his. Philip was smitten, besotted, and increasingly lusty. Full of dreams, he relished the shivery sensations of yearning. In no time, he would make her love him, only him, and then she would never go away.

Fiona was faced with a predicament of her own making. After saying she would marry him, planning to take it all back, Philip was enthusiastic. Then he put his hands on her. Resolve vanished under the heat of him. Determination sagged. She could not think, only feel his arms as she was taken away to happy land.

All her life she had lived with the usual story in her head. People met, properly introduced by trusted acquaintances or close family. A mutual attraction formed, of common interests, shared rank, or whatever. Fiona did not know. People were required to marry; it was the glue that held society together. Unmarried women were pitied and shamed. Men that had no wife were considered peculiar. To her knowledge, many titled men married to sire an heir. Women, to secure their future, have children to love, and a home.

All that had not tempted Fiona. Up to this point. Then Philip had sailed in, unusual, exciting, and beguiling, and three quarters of him was still a mystery. But he made her tremble with longing, for exactly what she was uncertain. More. More of all he offered. If this was some sort of dreadful hoax, she would die. But why would he want to fool her?

"You did not answer, Fiona," he murmured.

"Yes. Yes, I will marry you," she blurted before she could change her mind. Philip gave her such an intimate look, she blushed all over. "I am not afraid," she added for emphasis.

He came so close it took her breath. "Do I frighten you, sweetheart?" he whispered.

"Well, yes. And no. Can I keep my own money?"

He caressed her cheek, his hand warm. "Absolutely. Everything you own will continue to be yours. I will put this in writing, and practical girl, I will give you more. All I have."

If he was poor, that would do her scant good. However, Fiona did not wish to be crass. "I will share what I have, and we will seek our fortune."

Philip began to hug and kiss her, his ardor

apparent. *Maybe he does love me*, she mused, and if he did not yet, he would. She would see to it.

Things rather escalated. Philip bent over her on the sofa, abruptly a giant. Fiona sank into the cushions, dazed by his strength, his size, and by the passion of his kisses. He became more aggressive, and she quaked inside with excitement and fear.

"Fiona, I want you so much," he said, his voice husky. "Say you want me to make a little love to you."

She analyzed this request, and replied, "A little?"

"I want to touch your breasts and kiss them."

Her mouth went dry. *He says such things!*

"Here in this firelight, where I can see you. I want you to say that I may do so."

Why not admit the truth? Philip had. "I would like that," Fiona said, her voice shaky. "Please."

His dark eyes glittered and she was terrified, but the temptation was powerful. His arm around her, he put his free hand on her throat, moved it down to her shoulder, and ran his fingers along the neckline of her gown. He smiled and kissed her, caught the cap sleeve of her gown and slipped it down and down. The other sleeve went, as her pulse hammered. Her breasts were pushed up by her stays, and he cupped one, then the other, in his hand. She breathed rapidly, hot all over. The nipples peaked. He gazed at them, his expression reverent.

"Fiona, darling woman, how beautiful and fresh you are. I am humbled."

She relaxed a bit, then to her shock, he bent down, took her nipple in his mouth, gently squeezed the other breast, and sucked! Electric sparks struck through her body and she burnt to a crisp. "Ohmygod, ohmygod," she babbled, arching her back. The world altered in form, and Fiona immediately knew it would never be the same.

Philip was ecstatic. Her breasts were pale moons, rich and full, her nipples a youthful, rosy pink. No one had ever touched her, no one had ever seen her like this, naked to those satin stays that plumped her pretty breasts. Fiona offered them up to him, and he tasted and suckled her. She trembled all over. His virgin woman, his conquered maiden, would take him to the heights of his being.

He drew out her essence, tempting her. She shuddered as he kissed her mouth, invading her with his tongue, cradling her heavy, satisfying breast in his palm, the pebbled nipple firm and pleasing. She would give him everything he ever wanted, was supple, submissive, and naturally loving. Fiona Seymour would bless his life.

"I idolize you, Fiona," he murmured, righting her gown politely. It had only taken a moment to please her and himself. She must never be left alone with any man. None could resist her, and he would have to thrash them right and left. This would be tedious.

Her face was open and vulnerable, uncertain exactly what he had done.

"I longed to kiss your breasts, Fiona. It was a need I yearned to satisfy. This is not an uncommon thing among men and is enjoyed by women. Did you like it?"

She caressed his cheek, stirring his neglected cock. "Yesssss. And it raised other feelings. It was…oh, Philip, I cannot think when you touch me. I have no will."

Philip thought he would have some kind of attack.

His heart tripped, his spine tingled. The things she would give him, the levels of passion he would bring her to. Her innocent virginity was waiting for him to breach it and take them both to the heavens.

"I will make you forget any rules, Fiona. I will teach you to love me as I want, completely, with your whole self. I long to teach you about desire and abandon."

God, he had to get hold of himself, or he would not stop until he had her. Right on this sofa, on the carpet, standing her up against the wall. He was spinning out of control. Philip lifted her to sit beside him.

"I think," she said, straightening her skirt, placing her little slippers together on the floor, "that you are a dangerous man."

"I am," he replied. "You bring it to the surface."

She smiled wickedly, the minx. He had awakened her sexually. It was hazardous to leave, and more so to stay. He had played with her inner fire, and she smoldered.

"I should go home," he said with undisguised regret. "Will you think of me?" he greedily inquired.

"Oh, I will," she breathed. "I will. Nothing so— elevating has ever happened to me."

"I will take you higher, Fiona. I promise. Now, see me to the door."

They walked together, and Philip sensed a bond between them. Sex with her would be blissful. She was on the cusp of womanhood, and he would tip her over to the other side and sate himself. And she would do all he requested joyously. Allow him everything, and he would give and give to her. She would be the center of his days and hold his heart in her hands.

Sumpter was absent, and Philip opened the door. "Lock this behind me, if Sumpter is elsewhere. Be careful, Fiona. Do not leave the house until I come. Promise."

"I promise I will do as you say, Philip."

His brain soared, and he bent to kiss her, briefly holding her tightly. Then he walked out.

Fiona threw the bolt, as the butler hurried along the hall. "So sorry, miss. I was in the kitchens."

"All done, Sumpter, thank you. Have your rest. I will see you in the morning. Good night."

"Good night, Miss Fiona."

She climbed the stairs to her room, still feeling Philip's touch. No sooner had she sat down in the chair, Fiona's conscience tapped her on the shoulder. She should not have let him...do those things; it was horribly wrong. The rogue hypnotized her, carried a peculiar magic, and had directed it toward her with full force. He meant to convince her to marry him, then he would take her somewhere and, what did he say? Ravish her frequently. Was it a plot? Once he was done, he might sell her to foreigners, and no one would ever hear of her again.

Fiona clasped her breasts protectively and set off an avalanche of heated thrills. Nothing had ever felt so tremendous as his hands on her. His mouth pulling until she half fainted, making her want more. Her gown was lowered in two seconds. No wonder she had been warned never to be alone with men. They were crafty, quick to act, and so was Philip.

She stood and undressed. No sign of Daisy, but Fiona did not pull the bell. Better to be alone and think all this out. Tepid water was in the pitcher, and she washed her face and hands. Before the glass, she gazed at her naked self. Her breasts were full and heavy, her waist was narrow, and she did not have a fat bottom, the scourge of female friends.

Had Philip found her attractive? It seemed so; he was eager to taste and entrance her. And Fiona admittedly had loved it all. She was a scandal and put on her nightie to hide herself, turned down the lamps, and climbed into her bed. Chilled, she huddled in the cold sheets and knew there was nothing she could do to escape her fate. Which, it appeared, was Philip Laughton, the sailor. He had swept in on a tide of circumstance to lay claim to her.

Ravish her frequently, would he? She shivered and hugged her pillow. It would certainly be interesting, not to say sensational. She must find her way through this situation, keeping a wary eye. God help her, the ceremony might be real. Philip might actually want her to be his for the next fifty years or so.

Fiona mulled over all this, fretted, dozed, and before she was aware, slept.

****

Philip fended off Reston, who informed him that Cook was annoyed his lordship was not partaking of her dinners. The butler expressed anxiety that Philip would be discovered slain by footpads when not in the safety of the carriage.

"Thank you, Reston. Tell Cook I am swamped to the gunnels. If I will be at home for meals, I will inform her in good time. Things are in flux."

"Flax, sir?"

"Flux. Instability. Approaching chaos."

"Oh, my lord!" he cried.

"I am working it all out. Do not trouble." Philip strolled to the sitting room, poured himself a brandy, and drank it down. There was some danger he might explode with hot desire. His cock ached. It had taken all his resolve to walk away from Fiona. Her breast in his hand had been balm for all past cares.

How generous she was, how tentative and delicate. Her graceful ways had inflamed him further. He was a bloody savage. She in turn, was a vixen and a temptress in her innocence, and he was defenseless before her purity. But, thank the gods, she had an appetite for his wiles. Fondling her luscious breasts had rocked his brain. Fiona had appeared transported.

The liquor heightened his longings. Philip paced back and forth soundlessly on the carpet. He *must* have her. Some way, coax her through the ceremony. It would only take minutes to put her in matrimonial fetters, then she would be his. Velvet chains, gossamer bindings, so she would never go away and leave him bereft.

Philip was torn between searing need and a reluctance to bargain away his freedom. Freedom for what? The war? To be lonely into the future? He could not go back to such a life. He had tasted the riches of Fiona Seymour, and nothing else would do. Just get her through the ritual before she had time to think.

He would have her for his own after tomorrow morning. Then a wedding luncheon, to toast the event. With luck, pound Cameron to dust before Malrose seized the beggar and his cronies. Philip poured another brandy and sipped. As the drink scorched his belly, he revised his plan. He could not take Fiona to that appointment; it would be too risky. No, he would gauge the situation on his own. Go armed, in case Cameron got funny.

Philip trekked up the stairs to find Pearce waiting.

The valet closed his book and rose. "My lord. All is well?"

"Well and good, Pearce."

"And the arm, sir?"

"Redressed by my lady."

"As in a grievance, my lord?" the man joked.

"As in a new bandage."

He was helped out of his coat, neckcloth, and shirt. The neat bandage had held, and he was in no pain. Pearce took his boots, and he undressed, washed, and donned a nightshirt. As the valet gathered his clothing, Philip went to the chest and opened the bottom drawer. He took out a wooden box, opened it, and removed the compact pocket pistol.

It was wrapped in an oiled cloth. No rust, smooth action when he tested the trigger. The weapon was a product of the Americas, and he had purchased it from a tinker in Dover. It fired two shots. Pull the trigger, the percussion hammer hit the cap, and boom. Then cock and refire. That would do the trick, he reckoned, wrapped it again and left the box on the chest. He would load it in the morning and got into bed.

The valet turned down the lamps and inquired, "Will there be anything else, my lord?"

"No, thank you, Pearce. Good night."

"Good night, sir."

Philip welcomed the dark and took deep breaths. The lingering effects of the pneumonia were gone. His arm felt fit enough to take a bride. Could he actually talk her into it? He closed his eyes and saw Fiona's fine breasts, the nipples irresistible rosebuds. Untouched until he exposed them, pure, and chaste. Soon she would be his to discover and take unto himself. To indulge and please, to teach and cherish. He was thankful, nay, blessed to anticipate when—

No, he would not think of what he would do, what she would say. He would save it all to discover in the moment. Make it all last for hours and days. For always, if he had his way. Philip sighed, and in a drift of time, slept.

****

Friday

Fiona woke suddenly and sat up. What had she done? Philip was coming, and she had said all manner of crazy things. And she had let him—do not think of it; he will forget. It was probably a perfectly ordinary occurrence for a sailor like him. He would not mention it and neither would she.

She got out of bed and assumed a casual demeanor. He would not proceed with this marriage thing; it was suggested in the heat of the moment. She must take better care, Fiona chastised herself, and not get into reckless, um, intimacies.

A tap at the door and she halted, completely uncertain who was there. Then Daisy peeped in. Fiona released a trapped breath.

"Good morning, miss. I brought your chocolate."

"Thank you, Daisy." She took the cup. "I would have a bath, please."

Daisy turned to this task.

When Fiona raised the cup to drink, her hand shook. Must not get into a lather! When he came, she would say right out that she had only been—that she had not meant—oh, it was hideous. She had allowed such liberties, he might not even come back! He said all those things so she would permit—It had gone against years of training and smashed myriad taboos in five forbidden minutes on that sofa.

The bath prepared, Fiona eased into the water. The warmth touched her skin, and she endured an overall tremble. She had loved every second of Philip's hands on her. It was futile to lie to herself, to deny how quickly she had descended into a fervent space of being tenderly caressed. She lazily washed, thinking of it.

Philip had made love to her, never mind the circumstance. She had tasted physical affection with a fascinating man, a thing she scarcely knew how to grapple with. Fiona got out of the tub and dried off, Daisy busy assembling clothing.

"What gown shall you have, miss?"

Fiona went blank. "Um, the pale blue muslin, Daisy, please." Fitted closer, it had two buttons in the back. That would cut down temptation.

In her chemise, Fiona sat to have her hair done. Her face in the mirror was exactly the same. Ha, nothing had happened. Nothing had changed. Daisy was speaking.

"Pardon?"

"I was saying I would change the linens today, miss."

Fiona was overcome. Her throat filled with tears. "Oh, Daisy, you work so hard. I am truly grateful." She had all that money. "I want to give you a gift of five pounds, and five to Gregg, too. You both have been so wonderful to me. Now Father is gone, life is going to be easier for us, I promise."

"Why, miss," Daisy whispered, "truly, five pounds?"

"When I come down to breakfast."

She was helped into her gown, Daisy smiling.

Downstairs, Fiona went to the library and the drawer of cash. The room was very cold and smelled dank from the spent flowers. Fiona extracted two five-pound notes, vowing to always share her blessings. She greeted a smiling Sumpter and went into breakfast. Daisy and Gregg waited.

"Here," she said, handing them the monies. "We have had some rough times, but both of you have been tremendously helpful and patient. I could not have made it without you."

They appeared dumbstruck.

"My," Fiona said, going to the sideboard, "how good all this looks."

****

Philip also lingered in his bath but suffered no misgivings. Every part of his being was directed three blocks away and right into Fiona Seymour's person. He had some inkling that she would have an attack of maidenly guilt over last night's risqué conduct, but he would head that off. Darling, virgin girl, just let him have the chance.

Pearce handed him garments, and Philip dressed.

He probably should inform Fiona promptly of his change in station, but she might pummel him for not revealing facts sooner. In truth, the whole affair had been like running downhill too fast to stop. He had spent little time organizing his story but had just kept going. Telling Fiona this and that had worked for a while, but now he was in deep waters. He would get her to marry him, then when she was legally his, that is, if she would agree to have him, tell her all.

Never care what she thought; when he had her in his arms, she was pliable to a disturbing extent. He had to marry her or else tamper with her sensibilities. She was, after all, a lady of some rank, not a tavern wench, and deserving of proper considerations. He hoped all this made sense. He also hoped she rushed into his arms as soon as she saw him.

His arm was sore, but bearable, and the bandage was intact. The valet helped him into his shirt and arranged his neckcloth. Then he shrugged on his coat. Philip combed his hair, glancing into the glass. Was he deranged to consider marrying this girl he had known for a few packed days? But he had never felt like this, completely possessed.

As though, if he did not have her for his own, life would be ashes. There was nothing else for it; he had to keep on. It was like waiting for the *Calliope* to go down, bound to that wheel, disaster reaching out for him.

"Have you ever been in love, Pearce?"

"A number of times, my lord."

"And?"

The valet was philosophical. "The sacred waters tended to evaporate in direct sunlight. Passion faded. My way of life intruded."

"Being in service, you mean?"

"No, sir, a tendency to indulge in more than one woman at a time."

"I have only one lady on my mind. And I am going to act on that."

"I wish you well, my lord."

Philip tended to other matters, loaded the pistol, then went down to breakfast. He was ready to take a dive into the future, if Fiona would jump with him.

****

Fiona went to her garden and pottered about. An iris had bloomed, a lone white blossom topped the green stalk, and others were preparing to burst forth. She leaned to smell the faint green odor, and its ruffled petals were perfect. No weeds today, and she was careful not to dirty her slippers as she looked over the rows.

The finches in the elm tree warbled their song. The sun streaked down in rays that broke apart and scattered over the lawns. All was in order. Fiona went back into the house to wait for destiny to saunter in. How tall was Philip, after all? What were his other names? How did he live in Southampton?

She strolled idly through the house, disliking the furnishings. The hall clock struck eight times. Restless, Fiona felt she had been up for hours and returned to the comfort of the drawing room fire. She rather waited for the day to happen, so she would know what to think.

Was she so weak? How was she to direct her life, just sitting about? *Have you no occupation?* echoed through her mind. She had no training nor any skills but dancing and playing the pianoforte. The thing to do was get out there in the world, find a place, and learn to do something useful. What?

Marry Philip Laughton, came a quiet voice. He would fill her days, the handsome adventurer, to say nothing of the nights. She had enough funds to support him, until he found his way. Unless he heedlessly went back to sailing the dangerous channel. Except now he had no ship.

Fiona sighed. It was all so fraught. Her existence had caved in on her from the day Father had announced she must marry Cameron. Or had it? If she had not run away from such a calamity, she never would have met Philip. Never felt so light and free. She had not known how good his arms would feel. Or how tempting it was to let it all happen according to whatever he had in mind.

Face it, she was ruined in six different ways. The ton and its prim merriments was over. Maybe he would enjoy that cottage in Surrey she sustained her dreams with. They could—

This reverie was erased by the sound of Philip's deep voice in the foyer.

The moment had come, and she would have to decide. Unless he had changed his mind. She stood, ready for anything, and in he came. He walked toward her, and Fiona hurried to embrace him and look into his eyes.

"Fiona, darling," he whispered.

All her doubts flew away as he lightly kissed her lips.

"Philip, dear. How is your arm?"

"Much improved, thank you. How are you? You have survived last night's loving?"

"Well, yes, it seems I have." She needed to ask. "Have you changed your mind? About anything?"

"No, Fiona, I have not. Every hour I am more certain that to marry you would be heaven. Come and sit down."

They went to the familiar sofa.

"I have trouble seeing beyond the, um, ceremony,"

she admitted.

"Like most people, we will establish our life."

He made it all seem so simple!

"No one has a better chance than you and me to be happy," Philip continued.

"Even though our acquaintance has been so short? I must say, Philip, I know so little about you, and you know almost nothing about—"

The pocket doors to the music room opened silently. To Fiona's deep shock, there stood Cameron!

She and Philip quickly rose.

"Stay where you are," Cameron ordered. "And do not call out."

Fiona stared. In his fat hand was a large, shiny pistol.

Chapter Ten

Philip remained at his ease, his gaze fixed on Cameron. The idiot was in disarray, his shirt front torn, his cheek badly bruised. Another man appeared in the doorway. Philip recognized him as the fourth man at Maddox Street, the black hair, the short goatee.

"Put that gun down, you *imbécile*," he said in an accented voice, then smiled viciously.

"Good day. I must discommode you, Miss Seymour, and good sir, but there is the matter of certain monies owed. I am here to collect them."

"What money?" Fiona snapped. "And how have you gotten into this house, through the windows like bandits? What a fine pair of gentlemen you are."

"The safe. Open the safe," Cameron anxiously demanded. "This is a matter of—listen, he will kill us, do you not see?"

Philip remained silent.

"Give him the money, Fiona," Cameron now begged, the pistol shaking in his hand, "or else—"

The larger man reached out, took the gun, and struck Cameron across the face with it. He raised the weapon as Cameron began to sob brokenly, holding his bleeding nose.

"The safe, miss," he ordered.

"It is in the library."

He gestured with the pistol, indicating she must

come.

"There is nothing there," Philip quietly said.

"Silence. Move."

He followed, appearing meek, as Fiona marched through the doors, through a music room, and on to the library. She went to the desk and retrieved the key from the bottom drawer. Turned to the bookcase, moved aside the plaque, and inserted the key. Both men's entire attention went immediately to the safe, and they leaned forward. Unnoticed, Philip stepped behind the goateed man, his hand in his coat pocket, alert and prepared.

She swung the door open. Cameron gaped. The other man grimaced, his expression bitter, and turned to Fiona in a menacing way.

"Where is it?" he shouted.

"What?" Fiona asked, her expression pure innocence. "My father left me nothing."

The man turned to Cameron. "Deceitful English bastard," he sneered, pointed the gun at Cameron, who screamed, and fired.

Fiona lunged under the desk. Philip lifted his pistol and fired at the man, who went down in a heap, knocking over the containers of wilted flowers. Water spilled over the rug to mix with blood.

To add to the mayhem, two burly fellows burst in the hall door to take in the scene. Cameron screeched and wept, clutching his arm. The goateed man silently sank to the floor, gripping his right side with both hands. Blood gushed all over the place, and in hobbled Malrose.

"Ah, Monsieur Le Clere," he drawled. "So nice to find you in such distress. Take these two out," he instructed.

The hefty fellows hauled the bleeding men to their feet, Cameron weeping and in total wreckage. The Frenchman, bent over in pain, his thin lips clamped together, had nothing to say.

Sumpter, Gregg, and Daisy gawked as the men were dragged away down the hall and out the back doors.

Fiona emerged from under the desk, her green eyes wide. Philip helped her up.

"Colbourne, Miss Seymour," Malrose tutted. "I am most sorry about your carpet and this disarray. We have been lingering in your dining room. We were on their trail and knew when they came in the windows."

"We heard everything, Miss Fiona," Sumpter reported.

"They were spies!" Gregg excitedly said.

Daisy nodded vigorously. "Such a to-do!"

"Bring tea," Philip requested. His arm firmly around Fiona, he led her back to the drawing room.

Fiona held Philip's hand and collapsed onto the settee.

His men and the culprits waiting, Malrose took time to thank them and to explain.

"We have today rounded up the entire lot of traitors. You may both be assured this episode has done much to help end the war. Without funds, French defenses are disintegrating. Agents have been doing everything to raise money through theft, coercion, or any means available. Now, none of the amount we have recovered will ever reach French hands."

"There was money in the safe, but we took it to the bank," Fiona confessed. "Why was it here, and what had my father to do with it?"

"As near as we can figure, Viscount Greathouse took cash from a jittery Cameron, to safely hold. For what reason we do not know. Something to do with the purchase of high-yield bonds. Then Cameron was promised your hand to secure some arrangement they had devised. It is nigh impossible to sort out. Funds came from many quarters, as we understand, and are untraceable. I must be off. Colbourne, take your well-deserved rest, then see me in three months."

"Maybe and maybe not," Philip answered. "I may require a long recovery."

Malrose smiled, bowed, and hobbled out the door.

Philip gave her a hug. "You were splendid, Fiona," he praised.

"It was wildly exciting. I never imagined. And you carry a *weapon*?"

"If I feel the need to."

"So this is what you have done for years?" she cried. "Hazardous, thrilling! I can see why you have kept on."

"I have had enough of such skirmishes."

Daisy arrived with the tea. Fiona, amazed that everything was going right on normally, poured out, her hand steady. Gracious. Spies, guns, villains being shot in the library. The carpet would be cast out, and the thought made her happy. Then she considered what to do. How could she help Philip get through those three months?

"I have all that money, Philip. You could perhaps afford to—"

He cut in. "It is little enough for what you have been through. Save it for a rainy day. What about our plans?"

Her pulse thudded. "Yes?"

"Will you marry me, Fiona, or toss me out?"

Delight washed over her. It was the chance of a lifetime. "Just let me get my hat."

Fiona returned, a small straw hat on her rusty hair, her expression excited. The carriage was called for. Philip took care to keep her close to him, half afraid she would bolt. This was the most impulsive affair he had ever involved himself in, but he craved to have darling Fiona with him for always. He did not trouble to make heads or tails of it; he must just keep it all going forward.

"You are a beautiful woman, Fiona," he said, in lieu of any other inspiration.

"And you are a handsome man." She tilted her head and gazed up at him. "What if later, you decide I am not all you hoped?"

"You already exceed my hopes. Here is the carriage. Are you ready?"

"Yes. Yes, I am."

The faithful Sumpter held the door and they went out. He called to the coachman, "Number Three Colt Street, St. Anne Limehouse, Jem."

"Aye, sir."

Walsh held the door, they got in, and the carriage moved away.

"What is there, Philip?" she asked in a faint voice.

"An old church and a friend of mine, who will marry us. Fiona, I always wanted to marry you, Cameron, spies, or no."

She blinked. "Truly?"

"Yes. From the first." He must make certain

Lancaster, one of Malrose's men, knew his real name.

"Philip," she hesitantly said, "do you have some hope of...Is there a chance, after a time, of coming to care for me?"

It all tumbled out. He held her near. "Fiona, I love you with all my threadbare soul and will forever."

"Oh, Philip, I love you madly. Madly and forever."

They kissed feverishly.

The carriage halted.

Fiona stepped down to behold the church's white façade, the structure rising up and up in tiers to the bell tower. They walked forward, her arm in Philip's.

"St. Anne has a long history with sailors, Fiona. So near the Thames, ship captains would report here about occurrences of note at sea."

"Such a lovely building."

They went up the steps and inside great doors. It was cool, smelled of spices, and was deserted. Philip kept walking up the aisle, around the altar to a door, and they passed through. There, in a grassy space, a group of boys were playing ball, watched over by several men.

An older man in black saw them and smiled broadly as he stepped their way. "Hello again. Good to see you."

The men shook hands, as the cleric leaned closer. "Is this business?" he whispered.

"Not today. May I introduce my fiancée, the Honorable Fiona Seymour? James Lancaster, Fiona, rector of St. Anne."

He beamed. "How do you do?"

"I am glad to meet you, sir. It is a beautiful church."

"Thank you. What may I do for you both?"

"Marry us," Philip announced, taking the license from his pocket.

Fiona had the impulse to run for the carriage, tamped this down, and held fast to her reticule. "Please," she added.

The gentleman slowly read over the paper. Philip pointed to a line, and the cleric murmured, "Very good. Come this way."

They returned to the church. The rector retrieved a book from behind the altar, opened it to a page marked with a ribbon, and stood before them. "I am honored you have come to St. Anne. Shall we begin?"

Holding hands, they both nodded.

"Dearly beloved," he began.

Fiona's stomach dropped to her knees. *Do you, Philip? Do you, Fiona?* In a haze of minutes, her heart full, they were married. Philip took the gold ring from his little finger and placed it on her third finger. It felt heavy and warm; they chastely kissed, and it was done.

The register signed and dated, the rector was thanked, and Philip accepted a certificate. They hurried from the church to the carriage, climbed in, and kissed again. Jem waited for direction.

"Where shall we go, Fiona?" Philip inquired. "Somewhere fine for lunch? A little celebration?"

"Could we just go home?" she shyly asked. "And celebrate there?"

"Absolutely." He rapped on the roof. "Home, Jem."

The carriage moved forward, and into the future. Fiona, quite excited, nestled in the arm of her husband.

For his part, Philip was elated, hugely determined,

lusty, and triumphant. What did she think? This wedding was certainly not the dream of a ton girl, raised to expect St. George's, Hanover Square, a raft of attendants, and a gala. The carriage bumped along over the cobbles.

"Fiona, was the simple ceremony all right?"

She smiled brilliantly. "I thought it divine, Philip, the fine church, the nice rector, James. I never thought of a wedding, large or small. The last thing I wanted was to marry, my father prodding me, the choices unexceptional. Then you came along. I am more concerned with the after part…I mean, now we are married. Really married."

He hugged her. "We will have a grand time, you and me, Fiona."

"More loving?" she teased.

"Madam, I cannot wait."

She smoothed the skirt of her blue gown. "Did you ever, you know, plan to marry?"

"Never considered it. I was busy. Then you fell into my life."

They kissed, laughed, and kissed again. Philip was completely thrilled. Fiona was his wife, and he was a married man.

They alighted at Two Twenty. He had a thought to take Fiona to his house, but the image of wary Reston, the zealous Missus, and droll Pearce, was daunting. So few servants here, it would be ideal.

Fiona wafted into the house, the cheerful butler, stiff in his black garb, on duty. Philip followed.

"Sumpter, guardian of the house, you will be the first to know." She tugged off her glove to show her hand. "Philip and I have married, just today, at St. Anne

217

Limehouse."

The man's eyes enlarged. "I say! May I wish you every joy, Mrs. Laughton?"

Fiona clasped her hands together. "Mrs. Laughton! How distinguished."

"About that," Philip began.

"Mr. and Mrs. Laughton," she crooned. "I am so very happy, darling, and must tell Daisy and Gregg."

Damn if she did not walk off. Philip stood there. Sumpter's dark eyes rolled his way.

"Damn odd business, marriage," Philip allowed.

"As you say, sir."

"Fiona is a rare gem," he added.

"I would agree, sir."

Philip shifted his stance. "An eventful day, all in all."

"Yes, sir. The library carpet has been removed."

Thankfully, Fiona returned. "Well, Philip. Shall we have lunch?"

"No." He took her hand, led her to the stairs, started up, and she was right with him, step for step.

Fiona skipped along the hall, keeping up with Philip's long stride. She tried to look ahead, to anticipate, but there was no time. They were at her door, she turned the knob, and they stepped inside. Alone together, he set the lock. A line of tremors slid down her spine.

Philip smiled and took her hands. "Now, Fiona, darling. Do not worry about a thing. I longed to be alone with you. Shall we sit down?"

"Sit down?" she mumbled.

"There is no rush."

"Rush?" she mindlessly repeated.

He removed his coat and pulled off his neckcloth. Fiona was immediately energized.

"Wonderful. Let us begin." She boldly kicked off her slippers.

He took his shirt over his head. When she had tended his injury, Fiona had not considered the rest of him. The dark hair in a patch on his chest trailed down in a line to somewhere below the waist of his breeches. His skin was tanned or whatever, darker than hers. She swallowed, wishing she could be done with clothing.

Fiona filled the moment by kissing his shoulder. Then his chest. He reached for her buttons in the back and undid them. The gown loosened. The thin cloth fell down her arms; she caught a breath and let it fall. Philip put both his hands in her hair, the pins scattered, and it tumbled down.

"Ah," he whispered, took her in his arm, kissed her lips, and deftly unhooked her stays.

Fiona stepped back, took off the chemise and stays together, and stood there in her stockings. She bent to roll them down, as Philip sat in her chair and took off his boots. Stood and in one smooth motion, divested himself of his clothing.

Fiona's pulse sputtered. Mercy, he was gorgeous, manly, supremely tall, and well formed, with a very large, an imposing— Fiona could not recall the word, but it was highly intriguing, emerging from a nest of black curls, aimed right at her. His *member*, yes. She shivered all over.

"What a brave girl," he praised. "Fiona, you are the loveliest woman I have ever known. Will you come to bed with me?"

In the middle of the afternoon! How incredible.

"Yes. I will. I thought you would never ask," she joked, and that made it all easier. She moved toward the bed, conscious of her nakedness, but Philip lifted her right off her feet.

"Just a little lady, my wife," he murmured.

Fiona laughed, covered in bliss at the word, at this secret intimacy. Her room was shabby, but the bed was nice enough, and the linens were clean. He gently laid her down and climbed in after her. Here it was, life, acceptance, and at last, after all these lonely years, she was about to be thoroughly loved.

Philip guarded every breath and disguised his eagerness. They had taken the first steps, now he must accustom her to him. They snuggled together. He felt her tremble.

"Are you afraid of me?" he whispered.

"No, I am just—it is terribly exciting, and I do not know what to do."

"Follow your instinct. Love me and let me love you. This is all quite natural, Fiona, and I swear on my honor that I will never cause you distress."

"Should I say that I—that I have never?"

"Yes, I know. I have considerable experience, darling girl, so that will see us through."

"Oh, thank God." She sighed.

"But I would say, before we become involved, that I truly love you, Fiona. Exceeding any hope I ever had of finding such a magnificent woman as you."

Philip kissed all over her pretty face, her fantastic body within his reach at last. He paced himself, taking his time. Nibbled her neck down to her lovely breasts, the clean scent of her bewitching. *All mine*, he thought dreamily, and fondled them, nuzzling her pretty nipples.

She put her hands in his hair and tugged.

While she was distracted, he moved his hand over her belly and into her pubic hair, a rusty red thatch. Fiona groaned like the dying.

"Mmmm, sweetheart," he whispered, edging his hand down farther to caress the petals of her sex. Fiona writhed, and he loved it. "I adore every part of you." He searched for moisture, to gauge her arousal, and kept on kissing and nibbling her silken skin. She arched her back, and there it was, the welcoming wetness. Encouraged, he parted the fleshy lips, found her entrance, and pressed in his middle finger.

She went rigid.

"Relax, love, let yourself go." But it seemed there was no problem there. She raised her hips to have more and pulled his hair. He pushed in his finger and rotated it in a slow circle.

"Philip, Philip," she whispered.

"I love you, Fiona, and want to love you in all ways, everywhere."

"Yes, yes, yes," she cried, her whole body a virginal blush, so he went on. Found the sensitive nubbin he was aware of and gave it a little rub. She nearly jumped away from him but held on to his hair. He kept rubbing.

Fiona went limp, moaned, and came apart in a series of shivers, lost in her first climax. Philip congratulated himself. His cock enlarged and became insistent. She was soaking wet; he withdrew his finger and prepared.

"Say you love me, Fiona. Say you want me."

"Oh, yes, I do love and want you. I want it all, everything you know. Teach me, Philip, you darling, scandalous man."

She was so good-humored, Philip stopped worrying. Kissed her a dozen more times, placed his cock against her moisture, and chills went all through him. Then he got hot. A sort of mad frenzy overtook him; he had to get on with this or die.

"Fiona, my love," he murmured and pressed in a little. She melted, and the way was clear, so in he pushed. Jesus, the barrier. He steeled himself and pushed. Fiona yelped, and he felt like a bastard, but he was in, in more, and was home. He shook to his feet, and his head filled with bursts of stars.

Fiona was astounded by it all. His weight, his enormous size, his skin, and the things he did! It surpassed her shards of knowledge and felt like flying. Everywhere he touched sprang to life, and now, deep inside, how amazing, Philip Laughton belonged to her. The sensations were exciting; she could scarcely keep her thoughts in order, then—! She soared over the housetops, brimmed with pleasure, held on, and waited for more of his magic.

Philip pulled away, and she was shocked. Was it over? But no, here he came again, hotter, stronger, taking her over distant fields, over the river and far beyond to where lovers lived. He moved away, came back, and thrust with force. His hands tender, his kisses persuasive, his body satisfying.

Fiona kissed anywhere she could reach. Held him tightly and they moved together like dancers, like music, like every feeling she had ever considered. But she had not imagined this coming together, this delicate, sensual crash of emotions. This loving act stolen from the gods, who had kept their mysteries from her until now.

She climbed up and up, faltered, yearned, and was abruptly taken in a storm of quivers and trembling. Washed over by vibrations that tossed her across the sky, Fiona cried out in ecstasy.

Philip rose above her, gazed into her face, said her name and shuddered, his muscles standing out. A sudden flow of warmth within filled her with ripples of delight. He fell against her, and Fiona held him firmly. He was her husband, and now, she was beyond doubt, his wife. They caught their breath.

"Fiona," he whispered, "I hurt you, and am so sorry."

"Oh, do not be."

"All I can say is it was glorious to make love with you. Glorious."

"I agree. Unexpected, yet, somehow, familiar."

"You are such a grand woman. Nothing fazes you."

She smoothed his thick hair and caressed his cheek. "Most things do, but I just climb over them. You are tremendously wonderful, Mr. Laughton."

"About that. I have been meaning to say, to explain, that I have this title."

"Mercy, do I call you, what was it?"

"Colbourne. But I will no longer carry that name."

She hastened to say, "Well, never mind, I had trouble believing that earl business anyway, Philip, but it is all right."

"No, I mean to say—"

"You do not have to be an earl. I have lots of money now, and we can get by nicely until you find your place. I hope it is not sailing the channel and more spies. The war cannot go on forever, then perhaps we could take a little cottage. Somewhere far away from here."

"Wonderful. As it happens, I have a nice place down at Southampton. And a larger holding just up the hill has recently come to me."

Fiona became wary. This man! "All that on a sailor's pay?"

"I received no pay from the navy. I volunteered myself and my ship."

She sat up and clutched the sheet to her breasts. "Out with it, sir! Have I been deceived by a freebooter? With treasure hoards stacked up in Southampton? So! They took your title away, because you are a pirate? Then pressed you into duty?"

"Fiona, do I look like a pirate? Do not answer that. I am no longer an earl, because my uncle died last March, and now I am the Duke of Westonfield."

She covered herself further, yanking the comforter up. "How *dare* you tell me such a bouncer!"

"Fiona—"

"And likely, we are not *really* married, after I told *Sumpter*. Oh, oh, oh," she wailed, "I have been a terrible fool. Ruined by a scoundrel I hardly know. My father was right, I am stupid and worthless."

He tugged her back down with the linens.

"You are beyond riches, Fiona. What I said is all true, saucy girl. And I never meant to deceive you; I just did not get around to telling you things. I was too bewitched. I could not believe I had immediately fallen in love with a beautiful, vivacious woman, who was kind enough to let me into her life. We are legally and forever married. I am a duke, for what it is worth, and you, ready or not, are my duchess wife."

It all washed over her in a flood. Sailor? Spy? Titled? Did it matter? She loved him, whatever he was. Merciful heavens, he was so convincing, she always believed him! How could she control all this?

"Philip, you must tell me everything from now on. I do not care what it is. Excepting other wives, or unhinged children in foreign countries. Please tell me."

He stroked her hair, his amber eyes convincing. "And you will tell me, Fiona?"

"Yes, of course, I will. I promise."

"Then tell me I can make love to you again. Tell me you love me and will for always."

So Fiona did.

A word about the author…

I have a BFA in Studio Art, and spent my career as a painter and sculptor. I came to New Mexico from the east coast and began writing contemporary romance / mystery novels, set in a small ranching community near Santa Fe. Soon Regency period historicals captured my main interest.

I stretch the rules, but strive to portray, intelligent, self-aware characters, maintain a solid story line, and I include a cheerful amount of sex.

https://www.jeanettecollinshighdesertart.com

Thank you for purchasing
this publication of The Wild Rose Press, Inc.

For questions or more information
contact us at
info@thewildrosepress.com.

The Wild Rose Press, Inc.
www.thewildrosepress.com